Her Australian Hero

Margaret Way

LYRICAL PRESS
Kensington Publishing Corp.
www.kensingtonbooks.com

To the extent that the image or images on the cover of this book depict a person or persons, such person or persons are merely models, and are not intended to portray any character or characters featured in the book.

LYRICAL PRESS BOOKS are published by

Kensington Publishing Corp.
119 West 40th Street
New York, NY 10018

Copyright © 2016 by Margaret Way

All rights reserved. No part of this book may be reproduced in any form or by any means without the prior written consent of the Publisher, excepting brief quotes used in reviews.

All Kensington titles, imprints, and distributed lines are available at special quantity discounts for bulk purchases for sales promotion, premiums, fund-raising, educational, or institutional use.

Special book excerpts or customized printings can also be created to fit specific needs. For details, write or phone the office of the Kensington Sales Manager: Kensington Publishing Corp., 119 West 40th Street, New York, NY 10018. Attn. Sales Department. Phone: 1-800-221-2647.

Lyrical Press and Lyrical Press logo Reg. U.S. Pat. & TM Off.

First Electronic Edition: June 2016
eISBN-13: 978-1-60183-764-6
eISBN-10: 1-60183-764-X

First Print Edition: June 2016
ISBN-13: 978-1-60183-765-3
ISBN-10: 1-60183-765-8

Printed in the United States of America

*For the wonderful Diana Palmer with much love
and many thanks for all her kindnesses.*

Chapter 1

Alex walked quickly, even though the day was a scorcher with high humidity. A white-hot sun flared out of a sky that was bluer than any sea. The very air sparkled with heat. It sprang up from the rich volcanic soil, beating at her body, burning through the thick soles of her runners. If there were such a thing as spontaneous combustion, she thought she might go up in flames. She could feel the flush on her skin, but trusted in her daily routine of applying the most effective sunscreen on the market. Glancing down at herself, she noted the sweat marks on the red singlet she wore with a pair of denim shorts. These were her everyday work clothes. Once upon a time in the city she had been something of a clothes horse. Not now. She was back on the farm, and far too busy.

She had been out longer than she intended amid the green colonnades. R2E2, their second most popular mango variety, was bearing a bumper crop. The trees were laden with large, greenish yellow fruit that would quickly turn a deep orange with a lovely reddish blush. The heat had set the sugars, guaranteeing the fruit would be delicious.

The air over the entire plantation was saturated with a soporific fruity fragrance that made some susceptible people drowsy to the point of falling asleep. Everyone had heard of the term "going troppo." Another name for it was "mango madness." It happened before the onset of the Wet. There were no distinct seasons in the tropics, only the Wet and the Dry. She had always thought the name R2E2 was like something out of *Star Wars*, but the fruit had actually taken its prosaic name from its row and position in the field at Queensland's Bowen Research Station.

She had kept her meeting with the plantation foreman, Joe Silvagni, brief. They needed to set the date of the mechanical pruning that followed on the harvest. No relaxing post-harvest. There was always something that had to be done.

Alex and Joe worked in harmony, which was essential to the smooth running of the plantation. Harvest was a stressful time. There was always the fear of battering storms, hail, flood, early onset of the monsoon. Their top-quality bumper crop would be on the shelves from this coming November through February. It was estimated North Queensland and the Northern Territory would send to market eight million trays, with each tray packed to contain at least twenty large mangoes. Her own favourite and that of the entire country was Kensington Pride. KP had a unique flavour. The drawback was it was an irregular bearer with a relatively low yield. The September harvest had been disappointing, but there was always next year.

It was she who had given Joe the job, sacking the previous foreman, Bob Ralston, her father's appointee and a known slacker. She had endured quite an argument with her father about replacing Ralston. The good news was, in little over a year, Joe had proved himself. He saw all the things that needed to be done without waiting on orders from her or Connor. She and her father were meeting up with Rafe later in the day. Rafe's privately owned Jabiru Macadamia Plantation was one of the biggest in the world. Australia was the world's largest producer of the native Queensland nut, the "bush tucker" the aborigines called *baupa*. Not that the macadamia plantation that processed the delicious nuts through their various stages was Rafe's sole business interest. Rafe was an entrepreneur, just like his forebears who had ventured north from the colonised southern states, into the wild frontier that was Northern Australia.

Rafe Rutherford! Lord of the valley.

Some men cast a long shadow. Rafe Rutherford was one of them. She could scarcely remember a day when Rafe hadn't figured in it somewhere, whether in reality or in the caverns of her wounded heart. He had been hers and her brother Kelvin's idol when they were kids. The two of them had looked on him as the big brother they never had. Even their one-eyed father, Connor, could see past his adored son and heir to Rafe and the outstanding qualities he had in abundance. Their gentle mother, Rose Anne, had always had a great fondness for Rafe. In a strange way he still reigned supreme with her, if he only knew it, but their once idyllic childhood relationship had undergone a catastrophic seismic shift. That had begun twelve years before on the fatal day when Kelvin had been lost to them. At fourteen, Kelvin Ross had been destined never to grow old. Gone these many long years. Dead.

Past touch and sight and sound
Not further to be found
How hopeless under ground
Falls the remorseful day.

Kelvin *really* was gone, though she talked to him often, even if only in whispers. At the tender age of twelve she had been crippled by an overwhelming sense of guilt. She had continued to live. Kelvin had not. She knew better than anyone that if her father had to lose one of his children he wouldn't have agonized over his decision. He would have chosen Kelvin to live. Kelvin was his finest achievement, the apple of his eye. It should have been a daughter who died, not a son. The whole community knew it, though not one word was uttered in public. Everything was said behind closed doors. Kelvin Ross's death was a tragedy that lived in the collective memory of the town.

Rafe had always been extremely protective of her and her mother. Only she hadn't wanted that. She wanted it for her vulnerable, grief-stricken mother. Not for her. She shunned pity. Especially from her idol. Kelvin's death had stripped her of so many of her finer feelings. Guilt was her due. Death had been waiting for Kelvin that fateful day. She had sensed it without knowing why.

The close bonds between the Rutherfords and the O'Farrells, her mother's family, went back generations in the town of Endeavor. The two families had pioneered Capricornia. Both families had greatly increased their wealth during the Queensland gold rushes of the late nineteenth and early twentieth centuries. Gold mining had transformed the landscape of the State of Queensland. Gold had financed the building of Lavender Hill. The O'Farrell estate boasted one of the most beautiful colonial mansions in the state, so called because the house built in the eighteen sixties was surrounded by glorious lavender-blue jacarandas that protected the mansion like shields.

It was her O'Farrell grandfather who had deeded the estate to their daughter, Rose Anne, their only child. The estate included the house and the thriving sugar and burgeoning mango plantation. Her grandparents were returning to Ireland. Out of the blue, her grandfather had inherited a grand country house in the Irish Midlands. It came along with a minor title on the unexpected death of a cousin who had been shot dead in the wilds of Africa by an ivory poacher. A case of being in the wrong place at the wrong time.

Her grandparents had confidently expected her mother would return with them to Ireland. Instead Rose Anne had shocked them by announcing she was going to marry Connor Ross, a young man they had considered highly unsuitable. Deaf to all advice, the normally dutiful Rose Anne had stood firm. She was madly in love. She refused to give up the handsome Connor Ross. Seeing no other option, her parents had deeded Lavender Hill to her as a magnificent wedding present.

So that, then, was the way it was.

A sigh welled up from deep in Alexandra's breast. She still heard her mother's voice, just as she heard Kelvin's. She thought of them as silver bells pealing softly in her head. She had fought hard to block out her grief, though the scars remained. She got on with life. There was no other option. These days the great irony was her father couldn't manage without her.

By the time she was in sight of the house, her head felt woozy from the heat and the thick, pungent air. Her heart was hitting against her chest. Everything was starting to look *white*. There was no breeze to ruffle the feathery leaves of the compound's jacarandas that were on the cusp of bursting into an ecstasy of lavender-blue bloom. No shrieks from the legions of brilliantly coloured parrots feeding on the wealth of nectar-bearing flowers. A solitary hawk hovered above her head. It was waiting to pounce on some tasty bit of prey. She was so looking forward to the bliss of a cold shower before she started back to the office to go over the books.

Things were looking up. She had found four new markets. Two domestic. Two overseas. Her father had allowed her to take over the business side of the plantation in double-quick time. Over the years he had taken many unnecessary risks that had led to the plantation's financial difficulties. Under her stewardship things had made a marked improvement.

She had intended entering the house via the kitchen even if she risked running into Hazel Pidgeon—a surprisingly morose creature for one endowed with such a benign name. Mrs. Pidgeon was the woman Sasha had hired to run the house and do all the work. To be fair, she did it well.

Connor had married Sasha a scant ten months after her mother died. It by no means shocked the town. They were used to Connor Ross's ways. Except the glamorous Sasha, whom he had met on a trip to Sydney, was said to be some fifteen years younger than him. Connor Ross wasn't yet fifty and still a big, handsome man. Many women in the town thought so but were too canny to get caught up in his macho aura. They all remembered his treatment of Rose Anne, Alex's mother.

In the end, in no mood to contend with the housekeeper's seemingly permanent scowl, she walked around the side of the house, making for the front door. She didn't live here anymore. She had been virtually ejected from her mother's house. It had taken a couple of weeks to move into the Lodge on the extensive grounds. One of the few times she had allowed Rafe to help her. She and Sasha didn't get on and never would. Her father had gone along with the plan. That still didn't stop her from entering the house, invited or not. No one would stand in her way. Certainly not Sasha, a woman who Alex guessed had been on the make from her teens. She knew she had all the fight her beautiful mother had not. She had plenty of grit, but her heart was barred. She was herself, yet not herself for years now. She wasn't happy and she wasn't sad. She was *busy*.

She heard voices. Her heart flipped. The male voice was Rafe's. She would know it amid a hundred raised male voices. Sasha was cooing like a turtledove. Sasha thought it a secret known only to her that she was madly attracted to Rafe, but then so were most of the women in the town, married or not. Rafe was the alpha male. The utter embodiment of tall, dark, and handsome. He put life into every woman's beating heart. Not that Rafe cared about any such thing.

It was too late to turn back. Sasha had spotted her. No doubt Sasha's big blue eyes would be rejoicing in Alex's somewhat grubby appearance.

"Sandy! Sandy!" Sasha lifted a slender arm in greeting as Alex knew she was bound to do. Unfortunately it was all an act. An outsider might have been forgiven for thinking them bosom buddies.

She swallowed down her irritation. This "Sandy" thing was a game. No one, but no one, had ever called her Sandy, yet Sasha had hit on it from their very first meeting.

Petite of stature, Sasha had taken her hand sweetly, before making a point of standing on tiptoe to kiss her cheek. That hadn't been necessary; Sasha had been wearing very high heels at the time. Her brand-new stepmother had laughed delightedly, her eyes sparkling with mischief. Sasha and her father had been married in a registry office in Sydney, so the marriage had been a fait accompli before anyone knew, including her. From that moment on, Sasha made it plain she was the new mistress of Lavender Hill.

Alex mounted the front steps, appearing calm and self-possessed. Rafe rose to his impressive six-three. "Hi, Alex."

She had to wonder if there was ever to be an end to his hold on her. Was it even possible? His mere presence called up tumult. She gave him a faintly bitter smile. "Hi, Rafe." Their eyes locked. She wished she could cut the live current that surged through her body, but she couldn't. The force was too strong. Embarrassed, she became aware her damp singlet was clinging to her. She wasn't wearing a bra. She didn't have much of a bust in any case, but what was there was good enough. "You'll have to excuse me," she said, anxious to bypass the area where he and Sasha were seated companionably at the white wicker table. Its glass top was covered by a pristine white linen-and-lace cloth, embroidered at the centre and around the edges. Matching small napkins. Obviously from the trolley that stood a short way off, they had been enjoying what appeared to be a lavish high tea any tea expert would die for. Her mother's favourite Wedgwood tea service, Wild Strawberry, was on show. There was a silver three-tier cake stand holding what remained of a selection of delicious finger sandwiches—she spotted crab and cucumber—an assortment of pretty little cupcakes, and the obligatory scones. Mrs. Pidgeon had surpassed herself.

"Do stay and join us for a few minutes," Sasha urged. For some reason she was beating a tattoo on her teacup with her long, painted fingernails. An inferior piece of bone china might have cracked. "Take the weight off your feet. I'll ring for fresh tea."

How she hated these games! Never an offer of a cup of tea and a chat when they were alone together. "Please don't bother, Sasha. I need to take a shower."

"Of course, dear." Sasha smiled her understanding. "You do look terribly hot and bothered, I must say."

She was well aware of that. "That's probably because it's sweltering out there." Alex turned her head briefly to address Rafe. "You're a bit early for the meeting, aren't you?" As usual it popped out like a challenge. If she weren't careful, one of these days Rafe might react and put her firmly in her place.

"As you can see, I invited Rafe over for afternoon tea beforehand," Sasha cut in, as if she at least knew how to do the decent neighbourly thing. She was watching them with the utmost care, her light blue eyes darting from Alex to Rafe as though she believed some of the things she had heard from Connor were true. No one would question that Rafe and Alex were extremely aware of one another, even if there were no big smiles, much less hugs. Sasha couldn't recognize exactly what it was that simmered between them. Memories, she supposed. Heart-stopping moments. The death of Kelvin.

"Dad is out there somewhere," Alex found herself saying aloud, almost inviting Rafe to respond. There was an odd prickling at her nape and between her shoulder blades; an acute and uncomfortable sense of what could go wrong in life. "He's on his quad bike. I just hope he's wearing a helmet."

"He'd be very foolish not to." Rafe matched her tone with a quick frown. "Quad bikes put riders at risk. They're so unstable at speed, as we all know." He realized it was quite possible Connor wasn't wearing a helmet. Connor was a foolhardy man. Poor Kelvin had inherited his father's gung-ho attitude. He knew Alex would be thinking the same.

Alex!

As usual, whenever they met she stood alert, braced on her lovely long legs, resolute to keep him at a distance. He knew she had long since convinced herself that was the way to go. Certainly she hadn't unburdened herself to him for many long years. She had chosen to do it hard. It was a kind of self-punishment, he had always thought. Sometimes when he got angry—his anger was becoming more frequent these days—he thought of it as her ecstasy of guilt. Desperately in need of love and understanding from her father, Alex had been held at bay as if it were a sin for Connor Ross to allow his daughter to replace his dead son.

After the tragedy Rose Anne had tried her best to unite the family.

An impossible task. Alexandra, the young girl he had known so well, had been full of the joy of life. She could draw lightning-swift sketches of the people around her—many of him, to his surprise. She drew anything and everything that caught her eye. He remembered her many studies of the sylvan creek with its sculptural boulders, and banks overhung by trees that were a magnet for the swarms of gorgeous rainbow lorikeets. Alex had inherited her gift from her great-grandfather Rory O'Farrell, who had been from all accounts a fine watercolourist with exhibits in the National Museum of Ireland.

Hot and bothered or not, he thought she looked extremely beautiful and extremely desirable, as sexy as a woman could look without even trying. It was impossible to take Alex in at a glance. There was too much to cover: the flush over her high cheekbones, the flawless skin dewed with sweat. She had beautiful feminine shoulders. Beautiful small, high breasts. He could see she wasn't wearing a bra. The tight buds of her nipples peaked against the damp singlet. He looked away, his male body experiencing a near-painful erotic charge. What man wouldn't feel it? What man wouldn't want her? Alex had her father's height. Her mother had been a petite, small-boned woman. Alex was tall, narrow-waisted, with a strong, very slender body. One long, thick, lustrous braid of blue-black Irish hair hung down her back. Her vivid blue eyes blazed out of a face that wore what he called her regal expression. It suited her, he thought, half amused. There was a depth and dimension to Alex quite apart from her beauty.

Sasha Ross was a very pretty woman with a vampish look to her. Short, fluffy, curly blond hair, light blue eyes, a curvy, petite figure. Alas, no conversation but gossip. Certainly not issues of any weight. Someone must have told her men didn't like brainy women. Not true for him. Rather the contrary. Sasha couldn't hold a candle to Alex in any department. She could never have held a candle to the beautiful, tragic Rose Anne. What Connor saw in Connor's second wife remained a mystery to him.

"Don't let us hold you up then, Sandy. There's no real need for you to work so hard," Sasha said, wishing to show her concern.

"I can handle it."

Inside the parqueted entrance hall partially covered by a beautiful Heriz rug, she paused, wanting despite herself to hear what Sasha would say. "I just can't bond with Sandy," Sasha said on cue. "No matter how hard I try, she won't let me in."

The irony was she could have befriended a different sort of woman to Sasha. A nice woman. A woman of heart who genuinely cared for her father. Not an old-school gold digger. Alex stood very still, waiting on Rafe's reply before moving off.

"Perhaps you can start calling her Alex, or Alexandra, Sasha," Rafe suggested in his deeply attractive voice. "No one has ever called Alexandra, Sandy."

"I've only meant to be friendly." Sasha sounded hurt.

"Sandy doesn't suit her at all, Sasha. Her colouring alone, the blue-black hair and the vivid blue eyes!"

"Oh, she's good-looking enough, but she doesn't do much about herself." Sasha for once couldn't control the fierce flare of jealousy. "One rarely sees her in a pretty dress."

"Alex looks good in anything," Rafe said.

His tone told Sasha to move on.

Alex took the central staircase with its delicate wrought-iron scrolled rails that led up to the gallery, flying up the steps two at a time. She stopped at the top, thinking something was different! What? She turned. Ah yes! The big antique blue-and-white Chinese fishbowl painted with lotus blossoms and scrolling foliage, which had always held great sprays of orchids, was missing from the right of the stairs. It had to go back. Her mother had had great pride in all the Oriental treasures her family had collected over many long decades. Most of it had come from those trips to the former Peking. She remembered with a sense of relief when Sasha had suggested to her father making changes to the formal dining room. Her pleas had fallen on deaf ears. The walls were hung with a collection of Old Imari Royal Crown Derby dinner plates. It had been her grandmother's stroke of genius. The effect at night with the light from the chandelier glancing off the Imari colours and the rich gold decoration was entrancing.

Whatever the divide between them, it had grown immeasurably wider over the year she and her father had their hauntings. The house, apart from the kitchen and the bathrooms, was not to be touched. Her father and Sasha had not moved into the master bedroom suite. It had been left unoccupied after the death of her mother. She was sure if Sasha had her way, the master bedroom would be walled up. As compensation Sasha had been allowed to decorate another large bedroom, which she had done with theatrical skill, involving a lot of mirrors.

Alex had showered and was almost dressed in fresh clothes when Sasha burst into the bedroom without knocking. She slowly let out a breath, momentarily thrown by Sasha's entry. "Please come in, Sasha," she invited, "though a knock wouldn't have gone amiss."

Sasha's retort held unmistakable hostility. "This is *my* house, Sandy. I'm mistress here."

"Mistress? I don't remember my mother ever referring to herself as the *mistress*. It's your home, not your house, Sasha." She spoke evenly, but her blue eyes blazed. "You're my father's wife. That's the extent of it. I've moved out of the homestead to accommodate you, but I remind you Lavender Hill comes to me. I'll take over the estate when my father dies. My mother made him a lifetime tenant, that's all. This is O'Farrell ancestral land."

Sasha laughed aloud. "Ancestral land! You're joking, aren't you?"

"Do you possess some knowledge I don't?" Alex finished buttoning her blue shirt before turning to stare directly into Sasha's eyes.

"My dear"—Sasha's small, pert features were alight with satisfaction—"your father really should have told you."

"Told me what?" Alex whipped about, arching her brows.

"Obviously he didn't," Sasha said in a languid, theatrical manner, "or anyone else for that matter. But I reckon it's high time someone told you."

"Get on with it. Told me what?"

"Delighted to, darling. The fact is your late, sainted mother actually left half the estate to Connor."

The outrageousness of the claim took Alex's breath away. She gave a short, cynical laugh. "Sasha, that's utter rubbish. My mother made her one and only will with our family solicitor, Max Hoffman. That was years before she started to fall ill. Max read it out in the library after the funeral. What you're saying is preposterous. If there had been another will it wasn't made with Max. If Dad somehow had possession of a *second* will, he would have produced it at the time. Surely you can see that?"

Sasha made a half-agitated gesture. "I do, but for reasons of his own, Connor kept quiet about the second will and let the old one stand. He had very good reasons, he said. He knew he didn't have a particularly good status in the town. Maybe he was worried about reprisals—who knows? Your mother's family was just about lionized around here. But Connor told *me*, his wife, about it."

Alex's heart rocked, but she wasn't about to allow her anger show. "I suspect that was the big inducement. Sorry, Sasha, Dad was having you on. He's like that. He spins yarns instead of dealing with reality. The estate is O'Farrell land. It remains O'Farrell land. Even if you have a child, it won't be an O'Farrell, though I suspect you're not thinking of getting pregnant."

"I could well be," Sasha shot back, albeit halfheartedly. "Children are quite suffocating, parasites really. Tell me, did you *see* your mother's will?"

"Only you would ask." Alex began to brush out her long, unbound hair. It streamed over her shoulders, thick and lustrous, without curl. "Of course I did. My mother and I were very close. She loved me as I loved her. Kelvin was gone, but I remained."

"Anyone would think you're bloody royalty." Sasha sneered. "As for Kelvin! God, the boy's been dead for more than ten years."

"Twelve." Alex corrected her sharply, the taste of bitterness on her tongue. "I'd be very careful where you're going. The memory of my brother is strong. My father adored him. You are aware of that?"

"Oh yes. It's almost like a religion around here. Even Rafe won't touch on the subject, as if it's too painful. He was there, I believe?"

Alex held back a torrent of speech. Hadn't Rafe knelt, his long arms wrapped tightly around her, as she wept? "I'm not discussing this with you, Sasha. Neither will anyone else. You're a newcomer."

"Not so new." Sasha turned side-on so she could admire herself in the pier mirror, clasping her arms over her flat stomach, much as a pregnant woman delighted with her baby bump would.

"I don't see any callers," Alex remarked. It was unfortunate, but Sasha had made a name for herself in the town as "that awful woman." It was mostly due to her playing the role of the high-handed lady of the manor. Right from the beginning she had treated the local working people as her coterie of servants. Her mistress of the manor had been very much resented as well as endlessly mimicked.

Sasha's skin flushed. "They'll come. I'm not interested in the town people. Only people who matter, like Rafe. You do realize I'm only thirty-seven years old."

"Give or take a couple of years." Alex set her silver-backed hairbrush down on the dressing table. She gathered her hair to put it back into its usual thick braid.

"I assure you, I'm thirty-seven," Sasha responded as though flicked by a whip. "I could give your father a son. I've seen little evidence he adores *you*, his daughter."

"No," Alex agreed, her face down-bent, expressionless, "but he relies on me. I'll take that if it's all he can give. My father has always been an extremely hard worker, but he doesn't have the best business brain in the world."

"And you do?" Sasha's tone was biting.

Alex shrugged. "Listen, Sasha, lay off. I'm generally regarded as pretty smart. Lavender Hill is on its feet again."

"That's your calling then, is it?" Sasha snorted, her eyes whipping up and down the younger woman's tall, willowy figure. "To be a farm hand? Striding around in your tight singlets and short shorts. Personally I find your work gear too revealing, and to my mind unacceptable. Do you ever leave that plait out?"

"Woohoo! Is it any of your business?" Alex asked. "Do I ask how often you dye your hair?"

"Excuse me, my hair has always been fair." Sasha fluffed her short blond locks. "I see no reason not to touch it up. As for you! Wouldn't it be easier to cut that plait off?"

"Maybe my hair is my one vanity," Alex said. "A woman's hair is generally regarded as her mane. It's no bother anyway. Is there anything that actually matters that made you barge in here?" she asked. "I can't stand around talking trivia."

Sasha didn't need to consider. "You're wasting your life staying here. I thought you wanted to make a name for yourself as an artist."

That much was true. She did have a gift. From childhood she had shown promise. To her surprise, she had been offered a showing by a highly respected Sydney gallery owner. He had happened on a couple of her paintings in a Cairns gallery owned and run by a highly professional husband and wife team, English expats.

"Even I think you're pretty good," said Sasha.

"Thank you so much, Sasha. But would you actually know? As

an artist, I couldn't find a more beautiful environment than here. I have my plans, but all in good time. I try not to bother you. I keep out of your way. But you must know I love this place with a passion. It's been in my family for generations. My hope is that will continue."

"You might have to put away your hopes." Sasha bestowed on Alex a cold, pitying look. "Your father will do exactly as *I* say. He has rights. As his wife, I've made sure I've got to know all about his rights. I've impressed them on him. I've checked out where he might stand, even after all this time. After a good lawyer gets his teeth into the will, Connor's disgraceful lack of position will be acknowledged. I know all about contesting wills where there's a good case. Connor could sell up his share of the estate and there's nothing you could do about it. We can live anywhere we like. Stay in Australia or move abroad. The south of France appeals to me."

Angry at the intrusion, and Sasha's wild claims, Alex still had cause to laugh. "It would, but you'll never see my father in the south of France. Nothing will come of that wild idea. He doesn't give a toss about living the so-called good life. You'd never have the money, in any case. My father is quite simply a countryman, a farmer. I'm sorry, Sasha, but he has been teasing you about matters of grave importance. I'm sure he's become aware of your grasping nature."

"Forget the teasing," Sasha said, sounding enormously sure of herself. "Your mother did make a second and final will. Conscience, I'd say. Surely you can allow such a possibility?"

Alex whirled. "Look, Sasha, I don't have to weigh up theories. My mother didn't leave my father penniless. She didn't leave him without a home. She left him very comfortably off. Some people would say he got more than he ever deserved, but Lavender Hill is mine eventually. Rafe, who you so much admire, knows. The whole town knows."

"Not unless they attended your mother on her deathbed," Sasha flashed back, her small face bright with triumph. "What about her marriage vows? She, the devout Roman Catholic! She was mad about Connor. She probably loved him to the end, poor thing. What would you know? No one can get inside a marriage. Why, she even stayed in Australia when her posh parents wanted her to return to Ireland. She would have been the Honourable Rose Anne O'Farrell, wouldn't she? Didn't your grandfather inherit some sort of title?"

Alex wished now she had locked her door. "My parents' marriage is no concern of yours. It wasn't a marriage made in Heaven, but they would never have split up."

"Perhaps Connor lost the opportunity?" Sasha suggested. "Your mother didn't last long, did she? Early forties, for God's sake! Took to the bottle big-time. A crutch, no doubt, after your brother died. I do understand."

"You understand nothing!" Alex rounded on her. "You're unbelievably callous." She was trying hard to keep a clear head, but a red mist was gathering before her eyes.

"Your father blamed you, you know," Sasha continued unwisely.

Alex tried to hold back her sudden blinding anger. "Don't go there, Sasha," she warned. "You have no idea what you're talking about."

But Sasha felt an urgent desire to get square with her stuck-up stepdaughter. "Every morning to night, living with the knowledge you survived when your brother didn't. Must have been terrible. If you loved him so much, why didn't you jump in after him? That's what I'd like to know. I guess you turned coward, self-preservation and all that."

The speed with which Alex covered the space between them was awesome. Blue fire flashed out of her eyes. A red cloud bent her vision. She grabbed Sasha by the shoulders, backing her up against a wall.

"Jesus. Jesus. Jesus." Sasha cowered, wailing in shock. "What the bloody hell are you doing?" She was stunned by Alex's fiery reaction.

"I won't take accusations like that from you, Sasha, or your vicious remarks about my mother. Apologize."

Sasha made a low whistling noise in her throat, as if she feared imminent strangulation. "I'm sorry you find it so hard to answer," she rasped. "You should do something about your wicked temper."

"And you should do something about your cruel tongue." Alex removed her hands, only half ashamed of herself.

Sasha fell to taking exaggerated deep breaths. "The story I got was you left all the rescuing to Rafe."

Every word had the effect of a king hit. "Rafe was nearly seventeen, already six feet tall and incredibly brave. I was twelve. A small twelve. I didn't shoot up for a couple more years. I wouldn't have stood a chance. The creek was a roaring torrent. You might get to see it like that one day. Bring the subject up again, Sasha, and you'll wish you hadn't."

"Is that a threat?" Sasha was trying to appear untroubled, but she began to scramble away.

"Indeed it is. So take it seriously. I wouldn't bring it up in front of Rafe either."

"Oh, I know better than that." Sasha held a manicured hand to her throat as if it were badly bruised. "What I don't see is why you're so hostile to him?"

"Hostile? Who said anything about hostile?" Alex laughed, on the verge of bundling her stepmother out the door.

"You don't know how to behave around him," Sasha said, making her claim.

"And you do?" Alex gave a half laugh, freighted with meaning.

Sasha reared back like she had been stung by a wasp. "What are you implying?"

There was no mistaking the shock on her face. "Sasha"—Alex gentled her tone—"because I know Rafe so well I can tell you he has no interest in you. You're a married woman, for one thing, and there's no answering attraction. Please take what I'm saying seriously."

An unbecoming wave of red spread over Sasha's cheeks. "How can you say such things to me?"

"I may not like you, and you don't like me. But I don't really want to see you humiliated. And here's the warning: If I can see things, so can others. Dad would be extremely angry if you looked elsewhere. He could even throw you out. You may think you have his measure, but you don't. You don't know him at all. I should tell you my father loses interest quickly. As for his patience? It runs out even faster."

"There are certain things *you* don't understand," Sasha countered, licking her dry lips. "Why, you don't even have a boyfriend. Your father and I are wonderful together in bed."

Alex gave a disgusted half laugh. "I suspect you've learned a few tricks over the years. All those mirrors! It's a wonder you didn't have them fixed to the ceiling."

"We did discuss it," Sasha confided as though it was more about the asking price.

"And it didn't happen. You've been indulged. Only up to a point."

"You're jealous, Sandy. That's your trouble. I've heard how close you and dear little Kelvin were to their idol. Rafe's still your idol, isn't he? That's why you really came home from university, isn't it? Not to nurse your poor old mum-turned-alcoholic, but to get back with Rafe."

Alex felt the outrage in every fibre of her being. Her glittering eyes revealed it. "Listen, Sasha. You barged in, now I'd like you to get out. Fair warning. I don't know what I might do otherwise. We are not friends and we will never be friends. I came home to nurse my mother after her stroke, not for Rafe. Where is *your* mother, by the way?" she suddenly thought to ask. "You never mention her, or family, which I find very odd. Sasha, the enigma? You've never invited anyone here. You love showing off, so why is that? Is your real name even Sasha? Or is that an invention? Classier than the one you were born with, perhaps? I noticed from early on you didn't respond half quickly enough to Sasha."

Sasha appeared stricken. "What are you talking about?" she rasped.

"You must admit it's puzzling. I hope you're not a fraud, Sasha, though I wouldn't care if you called yourself Cleopatra." Alex felt vaguely surprised by the strength of Sasha's reaction, the fear in her. It sounded suspiciously like her stepmother had at some stage reinvented herself, shuffling off the problems that may have existed before. She turned away, the edge off her anger. "Oh, please go, Sasha," she urged. "You're tiring me out."

"You do know I can make you look bad with your father?" Sasha made a final effort to reassert herself.

"Don't bother. Dad isn't a man you can whinge to, though you've done your best from the moment you arrived. He just doesn't *listen*. He tunes out. Despite what you believe, my father doesn't take a lot of notice of women. He married you for the terrific sex you claim to have, not for your depth, compassion, spirituality, intelligence, whatever. I don't want to worry you, but think of it like this. You could be on probation. My father is not a religious man. He wouldn't think twice about divorce. I think you know that, deep inside you. You could have been divorced yourself, for all I know. We know so precious little about you. No family. No friends. No post. Maybe you get a lot of e-mails? You're a pretty woman. Hard to believe you haven't been romantically involved over the years. Even married and divorced, though Dad would have to have known that before you married. But it seems unlikely you couldn't find yourself a partner before Dad. You could even have had those clinging children, for all I know. Left them with their dad before taking off. It does happen. Lots of people go under the radar." Alex was literally making up a fairly commonplace scenario.

"How dare you!" Sasha was no longer in control of herself. "I don't have kids. I couldn't count my admirers from age thirteen."

"A real sexpot! Could we track any of them?"

"Why would anyone bother? You really do resent me, don't you?" Sasha said, backing to the door so fast she almost lost her balance.

"You bet! No offence."

The door open, Sasha managed another weirdly triumphant smile. "You'll be the one who's going, Sandy. Not me. Count on it. I'll tell your father what you've had to say."

"Go right ahead. Maybe you should start to consider that our past follows us, Sasha." Hard to believe Sasha was frightened by this new line of talk, but she clearly was.

"You're saying you'll have me investigated?"

Alex made the decision to back off. Sasha looked as though the gates of all kinds of hell might be opening for her. "I don't care who you are and what you are. Investigating you hasn't crossed my mind. Well, not as yet. My remarks were off the top of my head. No real intent, but they've clearly struck a raw nerve. You've been working on my father from the day you met. I bet you made it your business to find out all about the O'Farrells and Lavender Hill. There's plenty of information, coffee-table books out there featuring the country's historic homesteads. Now shove off. I've a meeting lined up. Oh, and I see the redoubtable Mrs. Pidgeon has shifted the big fish bowl that has always been to the side of the staircase. Tell her to put it back. Or I will. My mother had exquisite taste."

"Your sainted mother who drank herself to death." Sasha sneered. "Like your little brother, she is no more. Where is her jewellery, by the way? Connor said there was a treasure trove. Brooches, bracelets, earrings, rings, a sapphire-and-diamond suite you can take apart and wear lots of ways. Pearls, opals, a ton of stuff she inherited when the old lady died."

Alex's whole body had tensed up. She could feel pain at the base of her skull. "You're referring to my grandmother, Lady Carmichael?"

"Is that where you get all your airs and graces from?" Sasha asked with a snicker. "So where have you hidden it? Not that you could wear any of it around here. But I could."

"You? Get real." Alex didn't hide her contempt. "You're not about to be nominated the nicest stepmother in the world. Please go. We're talking *family* jewellery here."

"I'm *family*, aren't I?" Sasha hit back. "I married your father. That makes me family. Would you show me?"

The woman was actually serious. "No, Sasha, I won't."

"You're so bloody spiteful!" Sasha exploded. "Aren't you at least concerned for its safety?"

"Don't worry. It's quite safe."

"How can you possibly be sure?" Sasha persisted, as though she had a vested interest in the collection. "Anyone could stumble on it. Mrs. Pidgeon, even. Or there could be a break-in. Everyone knows the house is stacked to the rafters with valuable things."

"True. Only Lavender Hill's standing has brought something to the community, Sasha. The whole town is proud it boasts one of the most beautiful homesteads in the country. In my grandparents' time, and the early days of my parents' marriage, we had annual fetes here. One day I'll reinstate them. We've never had a break-in, Sasha. This is a very law-abiding town. My mother was greatly loved."

"Then it must have come as a big shock to this loving community to find out she was a hopeless alcoholic?"

Alex did some very fast counting to ten, shaking her head as if that might help calm her. "Get out, Sasha," she said tightly. "While you can. Don't come back. This is my room. I don't want you in it."

Reading Alex's body language, Sasha wisely decided to move. "If you've got any sense at all, you'll make peace with me, Sandy. I can be a dangerous enemy."

"I'm quaking in my boots." Alex all but flew across the room, banging the heavy mahogany door shut the second Sasha had made it out. Sometimes life seemed like a bad dream. She felt ill. She had known one day Sasha would get around to asking to see the family jewellery. She *was* family, after all: the second Mrs. Connor Ross.

The problem was, Alex had no idea where her mother had hidden the family collection. And hidden it she had. With her mother so ill, the last thing on either of their minds had been jewellery. Alex had assumed the many velvet boxes and jewel cases would be in her mother's wardrobe or at the bottom of the bridal chest, an antique Italian carved-walnut *cassone* at the foot of the bed. It had taken her months after her mother's death to even think of the jewellery. It was *there*. It had not gone out of the house. Her requirements were very simple. Only when she started to think about the pearls being locked away when they should have been taken out from time to time and worn next to the skin, had she conducted a quick search. To her dismay, she couldn't locate the collection. No painted trinket boxes, no velvet boxes, no Asprey brass-bound walnut box, the interior fitted with jewellery trays.

She had even asked her father if he remembered where her mother's jewellery was. He had taken that as a personal attack, and told her in no uncertain terms he had no idea. She had believed him. Neither of them had been in good shape. Neither of them had had a clear head. Her father in his way had loved her mother as much as he was able. He had recognized her goodness.

She hadn't *really* worried about the jewellery. It was in the house somewhere. She would get around to making a systematic search when she had the time. God knows there were many places to hide things in what was a mansion. Towards the end, her mother had been too ill and exhausted to speak of anything much. On powerful drugs, her mind had been wandering. Rose Anne had only had the strength to hold her daughter's hand.

Chapter 2

Rafe was standing at the veranda rail, his hands resting on the balustrade. He had a very elegant body, Alex had always thought. His wide shoulders tapered to a narrow waist, lean thighs, long legs. Just looking at him she had to endure the inescapable but suppressed excitement. That he had his back to her allowed her to catch her breath. His attention appeared to be directed at the long, gravelled drive. Clearly he was waiting for her father to arrive. He swung about, sensing her presence. "I think I'll take a walk."

She understood at once. "You're going looking for Dad?"

"Just going for a walk." He downplayed it. "Want to come with me?"

"Sure." She had to be demented, but at that moment it was all she could ever want.

"Where do you suppose he is?" Rafe picked up his cream Akubra from the circular wicker table. He settled it on his crow-black hair before pulling the wide brim down over his brilliant dark eyes.

"Joe hasn't seen him all morning," Alex said rather worriedly. "He could be taking a run around the lychee orchard."

His glance was so intent, Alex put on her dark sunglasses as a form of protection. "It's not been well managed, Alex."

"I know that. Thank you, Rafe," she replied curtly.

"You can't do everything, Alex. Your father relies on you far too much. You have no life of your own."

"At least my life *is* my own." Her mood was shifting to anger.

He surprised her by taking her arm. They were only a hairsbreadth apart. Her skin on his. She could feel the physical tingling. His grip seemed as thrilling as a caress.

"Your life isn't your own, Alex," he was saying. "Running Lavender Hill has taken you over. On your own admission you don't have the time for your painting. You've been offered a showing if you can get some twenty paintings together."

Startled, she pulled away. "Who told you that?"

"What?" he ground out.

"I've been offered a showing?" She was literally aquiver with tension. This was the dichotomy of their relationship. She had to have her secrets, but he wasn't allowed any.

"Sorry, was it a great big secret?" His expression said he thought she was being ridiculous.

"Well *I* didn't tell you," she stressed, taking off her sunglasses so she could better stare into his eyes. "Who did?"

"Alex"—he shook his head—"you're not stupid. Sarah Hancock knows. She does show your paintings at her gallery. She may have been the one to tell me. I'm not sure."

"It wasn't the woman who works for her, was it?" That woman, Gemma, was crazy about Rafe. Gemma would tell him anything he wanted to know.

"Am I supposed to look guilty?" He raised a brow. "It wasn't Gemma. Gemma never mentions *you*. Anyway, to get back to business. The orchard layout needs to be changed. It wasn't well thought-out in the first place. We both know that. You need to bring in an experienced horticultural manager or sell off that parcel of land."

"To you?" She flashed him an angry look.

"Who else? You have more than enough to be going on with. You need far more efficient cool-room facilities. Better packing too. I'll bring that up with your father later on. He appears to listen to advice, only he doesn't act on it. You know that better than I do. He pays no attention to good scientific practice. We have a big advantage in the Southern Hemisphere with our harvest ready for market when it's the off-season in the Northern Hemisphere. Customers are waiting on supply for Christmas and the Chinese New Year celebrations, yet supply falls far short of demand. I'd like that to change."

"You would, would you?" she asked aggressively. "Haven't you got enough on *your* hands with you and your partners trying to buy Moorooka Downs?" She referred to a giant cattle station in the state's fabled Channel Country.

"Alex, it's too bloody hot to stand around crossing swords." It was obvious he was trying to keep his patience. "Let me worry about my concerns. They're not yours. I never go into anything without thinking the entire project through. I listen to the experts. I take advice. I find the best possible partners. Look, it's too hot to walk. Get in the car." His Range Rover was standing in the deep shade of a tidal wave of deep-cerise bougainvillea, as spectacular a flowering as one would ever hope to see. "If your father is at the lychee orchard, we'll find him."

She wasn't about to argue. Not when the sun sat scorching in a dazzling blue sky. "Connor should be making his way back by now," Rafe muttered, once they were in the relative cool of the vehicle and underway. The air conditioning flowed in, a blessed relief. She set the vents so the air blew directly onto her heated face. Rafe reversed a short distance before turning onto the long, heat-hazed driveway. It was flanked in spectacular fashion by the beautiful native rainforest king palms. They towered some fifty feet high, having withstood many a cyclone.

"What else is wrong, apart from worrying about your father?" He shot her a searching glance. "Don't insult my intelligence by saying the harvest, the weather, the possibility a cyclone might be looming out in the Coral Sea. It's something else entirely."

She stared straight ahead, not at his long-fingered tanned hands on the wheel. His hands fascinated her, though; truth be told, she was supersensitive to everything about Rafe. To her shame she often had dreams about him that turned into sexual fantasies. A safe enough outlet for her suppressed, fierce longings.

Their proximity was pressing in on her. It was having an effect, whether she liked it or not. It had been quite a while since they had been in the Range Rover together. Not since he had helped her move into the Lodge. She had decided some years back, when she left for university, she had to put a merciful end to the passion she felt for Rafe. Passion signified loss of self. Loss of autonomy. She had suffered so much from loss she wanted to block it from her life. She wanted to block out her strong feelings for her childhood hero, however much it hurt her. "A mind reader, are you?" she asked.

"The answer is yes. With *you*." His tone, like hers, was on the curt side. "Is it something Sasha said? She was frantic to go after you back there."

"When she could have been enjoying herself, chatting to you."

His features darkened. "Don't waste time talking rubbish, Alex.

Sasha has no appeal for me. She married your father to take a big step-up socially. Or so she thought. Connor took her on, knowing it. Forgive me, but they're both opportunistic by nature."

"My mother left me the estate." There could not, *would* not have been a drastic secret shift on her mother's part.

"Of course she did," Rafe replied, in some surprise. "We were there when the will was read, Alex, need I remind you." Alex's mother, Rose Anne, had left Rafe a splendid bronze group of three horses. Sire, mare, foal. Rafe was well-known for his horsemanship and his love of horses. "She wasn't going to leave a share to Connor, now was she? Connor would have sold up in a heartbeat. Running the estate is beyond him. He thought he would have Kelvin to take over the running one day. He's using you. Worse, using you up. God, you even had to move out of the house!"

Alex had the desperate urge to unburden herself. She trusted Rafe's judgment. "Sasha told me my mother had made a deathbed will leaving half the estate to Dad."

Rafe shot her another diamond-hard glance. "Get real, Alex! And your father didn't produce it at the time? Leaving a share of Lavender Hill to Connor was something Rose Anne would never have done. It would have been a violation of her father's wishes."

"I know." Alex bit her lip. "Yet Sasha seemed very sure of herself. You could say triumphant."

"She was trying to wind you up. I'm surprised you've fallen for it."

"As unlikely as it seems, she claims Dad has told her a number of times about the secret will my mother made and signed on her deathbed."

Rafe all but growled. "Connor and Sasha have something in common. Both of them like to fantasize. Sasha is not the sharpest knife in the drawer, and I would wager she's a habitual liar. Either Connor managed to totally fool her, or she was only trying to rattle your cage. There *was* no second will. It didn't happen. Who would the witnesses have been? I can't think of a soul who would witness such a will. Max knows nothing about this alleged second will that Connor for some incredibly obscure reason withheld."

"You don't think Dad could have convinced her while she lay dying?" Alex asked, suddenly fearing a remote possibility. "They were husband and wife, after all. She had loved him madly, remember. Women do continue to love the wrong man. My mother was very religious. She may have felt it her duty. I wasn't at her bedside all the time, you know. I had to get *some* sleep."

Rafe's tone turned supportive. "Alex, your mother couldn't have had a more devoted, loving daughter. We both know your father shunned the sickroom. He had a near pathological horror of sickness. He couldn't handle your mother's illness. I don't buy this nonsense Sasha decided to spring on you. Your father had his own reasons for selling Sasha a fantasy. He would have seen her gullibility. He could even have been testing her. Sasha is a grasping woman. To the entire North, this is O'Farrell land, pioneered by the O'Farrell family."

"Maybe Dad and Sasha have hatched some sort of plan?" Alex persisted, trying to figure out reasons for Sasha's out-of-the-blue disclosure. "There are countless examples of bitter disputes over wills. We both know that. Lawyers get rich handling the affairs of battling parties."

"Kill the lawyers first." Rafe only half joked. "At the end of the day, didn't the Palmers have to hand over most of their inheritance to their lawyers? Connor never breathed one word about another will. Ergo, there wasn't one. If your mother had made a new will, Connor would have produced it at the time. The one and only will was read by Max without a peep out of Connor."

"It doesn't make sense, I know," Alex said, "unless Dad kept quiet about another will because he needed me. He needed my skills in the house and the estate. It suited him to let things lie. Maybe he thought he could contest the will at some time in the future. He could come up with extenuating reasons to put to the court. Claim the adverse effects on him. He lost a good deal of the money Mum left him. He made so many mistakes. Who knows what he might do now, when I'm running the estate? To outsiders, to the court, my mother's will might seem unfair. Dad has standing as her husband of over twenty years. Father of their two children. Hard worker for the estate. He could claim he was her prime carer when she fell ill, and she was ill for a long time."

Rafe was silent for a moment, thinking hard. "Alex, I don't know the answers to all of this. Max will. Disputes through the courts cost a fortune. Your grandparents had valid reasons for not trusting Connor with any part of the estate. The plantation would have failed. My family would have bought Lavender Hill in a tick."

"Don't I know it!" she said as though angered by the idea.

Rafe held on to enough patience to reply. He looked out the window at the swaying palm fronds. "Many years ago my family had already begun to hope for a union between our two families. My mother especially was very keen on it."

"You and me?" Alex burst out before she could stop herself. "Are you talking about you and me? I was only a child."

He shrugged a shoulder. "Children grow up. We were great friends once, Alex. You can't have forgotten."

"I haven't forgotten. Kel and I adored you," Alex said, fighting down emotion. "You were our hero. We followed you everywhere, don't you remember? You risked your life to save Kelvin. I'll never forget that to my dying day."

"So how then do you explain the alienation?"

For a moment she looked at him without answering. "You're better off not knowing."

"Better yet, how can you tell me when you're not fully aware of the reason yourself?"

"I don't want to talk about it, Rafe." She knew he wasn't taking her attitude well.

"That's your big problem, Alex. You need a ticket *back* to life. You've been running on the wrong track. It's high time you hopped off. There have been close bonds between the Rutherfords and the O'Farrells going back generations. We pioneered this part of the world. Our families have always been friends and neighbours. We were always there for your mother. Connor too, for that matter. He was always coming to Dad for advice. The pity was he never took it."

"Your father was the kindest and most generous of men," she said, remembering with sadness how Rafe's father, Ralph, with two other passengers, had been killed in a light airplane crash over New Guinea, a dangerous place to fly over at any time, several years before. Rafe's mother, Laura, now lived in London near her daughter, who was married to a career diplomat. Rafe had endured his tragedies just like she had. Only he had coped so much better.

"The last thing any of us wants is for you to keep punishing yourself, Alex. Don't forget me in the process. As for Sasha, if you're so concerned about her fanciful allegations, talk to your father about it."

"I can't talk to Dad about anything," she said, her expression downcast. "We don't have a normal relationship."

Rafe groaned. "Hard to know which one of you has built the higher wall. Your father isn't a happy man, Alex, second marriage or not. He married Sasha on sexual impulse—not romantic love. Anyone can see that. She would have played up to him. Big-time. He needed that to restore his self-confidence. Connor talks big but he doesn't *feel* big. That's the trouble. Marrying Sasha hasn't proved to be enough. I don't think he'd notice if Sasha went off one day and never returned."

Alex was genuinely startled. "You really mean that?"

"I can read your father, Alex. Another man, I suppose. He probably opens up more to me than you. One of his forms of escape is like today, racing around the estate on that quad bike."

"It worries me," she said bleakly.

He nodded. "And me. Connor knows all about the spate of accidents, but he somehow believes that can't happen to him. He puts great store in his physical abilities."

Everyone who knew her father had spotted that. "It's the big concern." She could only hope and pray her father's stubborn adherence to risk-taking didn't one day catch him out.

They reached the orchard. In the steamy light it looked green and luxuriant. The trees with their interlocking canopies stood a uniform twelve feet high, bushy but not as vigorous as they should be. They carried a harvest of Kwai May Pink, which was clearly ready for picking. At the end of one corridor, through the white-gold heat haze, they spotted a farm employee on a tractor. He disappeared from sight. It wasn't Connor Ross.

"Let's get out," Alex said tersely, already opening the door.

"Try to relax," Rafe urged when he joined her. His striking face appeared to be all planes and angles, his tension apparent. It had to be the heat. She felt half crazy herself. "Everything will hurt less if you relax."

Her vivid blue eyes were intent on his face. "Words to live by, are they? The biggest mistake I could ever make now is relax with *you*." She hadn't meant to say anything remotely provocative, only the words had burst out, convulsively.

"And why is that?" Rafe retorted. He rounded on her with his vastly superior strength and height. No wonder women feared men and their physicality, she thought, not that she had any fear of Rafe. Consequently she didn't take one step back from him. "Let's concentrate on finding Dad, shall we?"

"Let's concentrate on you finding *you*," Rafe retaliated, his tone grating. "Can you open your heart to anyone anymore? Or have you totally lost the key? I'm sick of watching you dig yourself deeper and deeper into a black hole. You're desperate to keep me at arm's length. It's almost a form of torture. For God's sake, can't you tell me why? You've carried a terrible burden of irrational guilt. I know that better than anyone. But surely it's about time you put it down. Or do you feel compelled to *wallow* in it?"

Neither of them could say later who acted first. Anger rushed at them with lightning speed. Alex's hand flew up to strike the look of high scorn on Rafe's smouldering face, just as Rafe moved to pull her to him, crushing the length of her body against his. There was no question of pausing, of catching breath. Both of them, always on the thin edge of control, lost it. Lost whatever it was that had kept them in check.

Rafe's mouth came down over hers with an insatiable hunger. One hand came up to cup the swell of her high breast, his thumb and forefinger working the already erect nipple. It was a colossal assault on the senses. A button loosened under siege, popped off her shirt. Immediately his hand slipped further inside her top while she gasped out whimpers she couldn't control at the sensual ecstasy he was arousing in her. This was too devastating to be called lovemaking. It was a desperately harsh and hurtful *want*. In another minute they would be down on the thick grass, high on a sexual attraction so powerful the immediate world would fall away in a brilliant blur.

It was Rafe who came to first, keeping one hand on her arm as she rocked unsteadily on her feet. His voice crackled like an overloaded circuit. "You had that coming."

She had to believe it. Her blue shirt was curled up around her waist, most of the white pearly buttons undone. With unsteady fingers she rebuttoned it, covering her breasts. "I won't, I *don't,* I *refuse* to love you, Rafe."

"Who said anything about love," he mocked, burning with a kind of sexual electricity held powerfully in check. "If you won't allow us to communicate with our souls, I guess our bodies will have to do. I'll settle for being your lover. Who cares about a soul mate?"

She did, but she wasn't going to show it. "You can say goodbye to that idea."

He burned her with his eyes. "Until the next time," he told her. "We'll do it one step at a time."

"Should I start keeping a diary? You're incredibly arrogant, Rafe." She bent forward slightly as shock waves continued to run through her.

"I have to reject that. I've been incredibly patient with you, Alex. Only now you've given yourself away in one fell swoop. You don't love me, but you're mad for me to make love to you. You needed that as much as I did."

It was impossible to reassemble herself. "Animal magnetism," she said, struggling to airbrush the moments of high emotion out of her mind. "That's all it was. Animal magnetism."

"I'm cool with that." His tone was sardonic. "At least it got you flying into my arms."

"And not much chance of it happening again."

He didn't appear impressed. "Words are toys, Alex. They're only meant to be fun. Let's go back to the house. I'll take the Long Walk. I know your father goes there often. Unlike you."

"And *you*. We can never go back to what we were, Rafe."

"Okay, we can't. What we do, is take a new direction. I want you, Alex. Let there be no mistake about that."

"When I've got nothing to offer you?" She stared up at him with great intensity. Several strands of hair from her braid hung loose, blue-black against her glimmering skin. Her full mouth burned crimson.

"I'll take what I can get. No matter how hard you try, Alex, you'll never succeed in locking me out."

They had driven more than halfway down the broad grassy corridor the family had always called the Long Walk. It bordered the entire length of the creek that on that afternoon was one sparkling green ribbon, shot with silver. About fifteen yards off they saw one of the farmhands lumbering towards them like he was completely out of breath, yet he was waving his hands frantically in the air.

"Here's trouble!" Rafe announced grimly, pulling the Range Rover onto the verge.

Alex froze. The scarlet-faced farmworker had almost reached them, shouting at them in Italian.

Reared in the North with its big population of Italian descendants, both Alex and Rafe were quite fluent in Italian. There had been a terrible accident involving "Mr. Connor! Mr. Connor!"

Another vehicle was racing down the Long Walk, honking madly. It swerved around Rafe's Range Rover, coming to a halt beneath the overhanging trees. Joe Silvagni jumped out, looking severely shaken. He joined Alex and Rafe who had gotten out of the car as well. He had received the message a few moments before. Connor Ross was pinned under his quad bike at the Three Mile. He was alive. He was wearing his helmet, which had probably saved his life, but there were injuries.

"Let's get there." Rafe turned to order the exhausted farmhand into the back of the Range Rover. "Get going, Joe," he called to the estate foreman. "We'll follow."

"Right, boss." Joe pulled out, driving away so fast, his tyres sent up spumes of dust and grass into the air. They all realized this was a life-and-death situation. The O'Farrells, so highly regarded in their part of the world, were not a family that lived happily ever after.

Alex shot an anxiety-ridden glance at Rafe. Her body was sending out powerful alarm signals. Her legs felt as though they could give way. "Someone will have to tell Sasha."

"I'll organize it." Rafe turned his back, pulling out his mobile.

Sasha, for good or bad, was her father's wife. She had rights.

"Well?" she asked when Rafe came back to her. Sasha would have to take her own car, she thought. There was no time to go back to the house.

"For God's sake, Alex, get in the car." It was another order, quick and hard.

She obeyed. The prospect of another family loss had been brought terrifyingly into the present. The air conditioning came back on full blast. She had never fainted in her life, but there was always a first time.

The ambulance came on the tragedy in double-quick time. The three men had lifted the quad bike off Connor Ross, who was mercifully unconscious, but it was obvious to them all he had been very badly injured with God knows how many breakages and internal injuries.

Alex stood a little way apart, swallowing hard. Surely there had been far too many deaths in her life. Tragedy seemed to surround her. Kelvin had died at the age of fourteen. Her mother had died at the age of forty-two, her health destroyed by grief and an addiction to alcohol; prior to the death of her only adored son, she hadn't drunk at all. A glass of champagne at Christmas, but even then she hadn't finished off the glass. Grief tipped people over the edge. The loss of a beloved child was the greatest grief any woman could be called on to bear.

Now her father. She *knew* her father was going to die. The paramedics weren't saying. No one was speaking. They all studied Connor Ross's broken body in silence. Her father had always claimed quad bikes were "as safe as houses," even though quad bikes had taken over tractors as the leading cause of accidental deaths on farms. Her father had always been a reckless man, flying around the estate when she had spoken to him many times about his bike's instability at speed and over uneven ground.

Rafe materialized by her side. She felt the grip of his hand on her shoulder. "We'll follow on to the hospital."

"He's not going to survive, is he, Rafe?"

Rafe's grip tightened. "Such a senseless waste."

"Death is like an eagle's claws, isn't it?" she said, sunk in despair. "It never releases its grip. We both tried to warn Dad, didn't we?"

"Don't dwell on it, Alex. Your father went his own way in all things. He did *not* listen. He said many times he couldn't run the plantation without his bike. A lot of farmers still swear by them. Most would never be as reckless as Connor was."

"Didn't we catch glimpses of the recklessness in Kelvin? Dad passed that rashness on to Kelvin." Her memories caught her vividly. "I screamed at him not to dive off the rocks. I screamed myself hoarse. You heard me. Kel didn't take a scrap of notice, to my unending sorrow. Then you came out of nowhere. You tried to save him when you could have been killed yourself."

Rafe himself wasn't at peace with Kelvin's death. "Someone up there wanted us both alive," he said gravely.

"The gods make us part of the game. Sasha practically called me a coward for not jumping in."

"Stupid woman!" Rafe muttered beneath his breath. "She's not coming, by the way. Claims she's too distraught."

"What?" Even knowing Sasha as she did, Alex was still shocked.

"She hates hospitals. She doesn't want to see her husband all smashed up, a possible paraplegic. I did remind her she had vowed to love and cherish him. Couldn't help it. I don't think Sasha is a totally genuine human being, let alone a loving wife."

"Well, today she might find herself a widow." A rich widow, expecting to inherit at least part of an historic estate from her late husband, Alex thought. It looked very much like whatever feeling Sasha had had for her husband was fast becoming a memory. Not that she believed for one moment Sasha had loved her father. Even more extraordinary, she had never felt her father had loved Sasha. Sasha was no more than a trophy. Alex's heart contracted at the thought of her father paralysed, confined to a wheelchair. He had always been a vigorous man with no health problems to speak of. She was so lightheaded with shock, she was moving beyond distress.

"You okay?" Rafe shot a keen glance at her.

"I don't know what I am," she said, making a funny little gesture of powerlessness.

"We'll get through this, Alex. We've done it before. We'll do it again."

When they arrived at the hospital they were greeted in the corridor by George McCreight, the senior doctor. They both knew him well. McCreight's face said it all. Connor had passed away of multiple injuries to his stomach, chest, spine, as well as fractured limbs, before they could get him to surgery. He had never regained consciousness. On all of their minds was the number of deaths and serious injuries that had occurred on rural properties of late. A young girl had been killed a few months previously when she had been thrown off her speeding bike, not wearing her protective helmet.

They sat close together on a hospital bench, Alex staring blindly at her shaking hands. "I loved my father, but he didn't love me. That's kind of sad, isn't it?"

"It puts an intolerable weight on a child's heart," Rafe said, with an uncontrollable flash of anger towards Connor Ross. His callous treatment of his daughter, his only living child, had been universally condemned.

"God, this can't be happening." Alex groaned, dropping her head towards her lap.

"It is happening, I'm afraid. Leave your head down for a while, Alex." Rafe's fingers closed over her nape.

"It's okay. I'm all right," she said after a minute. "Would you ring Sasha? I can't."

"I've already rung her."

Alex lifted her head. "How did she react?"

"Shocked." In actual fact Sasha hadn't reacted as if she had been delivered a great blow. It had been more like a call to abandon ship.

Glancing down the hospital corridor, Rafe warned, "People are arriving." A group of friends from the town was fast approaching. "The news is already out. Think you can handle this?" he asked quickly. "If you can't, I'll head them off."

Alex made a visible effort to pull herself together. She sat up straight, squaring her shoulders. "No, it's okay. These are good people. I promise I won't cry. I'll cry later."

"Oh, Alex," Rafe groaned. It was a cry from the heart. There was no pattern to life, he thought. No plan. Things came out of the blue. Good things. Bad things. He wondered why he wasn't as shocked at Connor's death as he should have been.

"Oh, Alex, Alex, we're all so sorry." Kylie, the lovely little seven-year-old daughter of a mutual friend, bounded up to Alex, throwing her arms around her and hugging her tight.

Kylie started to cry so hard Alex found herself turning into the comforter. "There, there, Kylie."

There wasn't a single person who didn't hold Alexandra Ross in the highest regard. Just as at the death of her mother the town had turned out for her, the town would be there for Alex again, supporting her in yet another difficult, highly emotional time.

Rafe doubted Alex would get much support from her stepmother. More stormy times ahead, he thought grimly. He wondered what nonsense Sasha had been talking about—a deathbed will, which Connor, for some obscure reason, had kept secret. Connor had always been a man who liked to talk himself up. One thing Rafe knew: Lavender Hill Estate was going to stay intact for Alex.

There was to be more drama when they returned to the homestead. They arrived at the front door to the sight and sound of a Louis Vuitton suitcase crashing down the staircase. All of the exterior and most of the interior lights were blazing, as if Sasha were terrified of being alone in a dark house.

"What's going on?" Alex moved swiftly into the entrance hall. "Sasha?" she called, her voice full of urgency.

Sasha appeared from off to the right of the staircase, looking bone-white. She stared back at Alex and Rafe, transfixed.

"What is it? What's happening here, Sasha?" Rafe asked.

"I can't stay here," she cried, as though they were about to prevent her from leaving by force if need be. "I'm going into town. I've taken a room at the motel."

"You've what?" Alex had yet to meet someone like Sasha.

"If I were in your shoes, I'd stay here," Rafe told Sasha crisply.

"I'll stay with you, Sasha," Alex quickly offered, "if being alone is worrying you." Sasha did look overcome by fear. "You don't need to be alone in the house."

"No one can make me. I'm going *now*!" Sasha cried. "There are ghosts here. Too many ghosts." She was scrabbling and losing her grip on her suitcase. "They all hate me."

"You're quite clear about what you're doing, Sasha?" Rafe asked. "You weren't present at the hospital, and now you propose to stay in town. People talk."

"Of course they do!" she flashed back. "I know I'm not liked. My taxi will be here in a moment. You can't stop me, Rafe."

"No one will stop you, Sasha," Alex broke in. "But Rafe is right. The town will find it pretty odd."

"Bugger the town!" Sasha cried fiercely. "They would question anything I did." Her fluffy blond head shot up. "That will be the taxi now." Clearly she was in a tremendous hurry to leave.

"The funeral will be at the end of the week," Rafe bit out. He had made any number of necessary phone calls on Alex's behalf in this terrible situation.

A storm of fright showed in Sasha's white face. "I don't know if I can make that either. I hate funerals. I didn't take this on, you know, losing a husband after barely a year. It's not the way it was supposed to be."

"No," Alex agreed, biting down hard on her lip.

Sasha abruptly turned businesslike. "I'll be back to hear the will read, of course." Her eyes bored into Alex's. "You're in for some contest, Sandy. Better prepare yourself."

"Is that the best you're capable of?" Rafe's voice was like tempered steel. He moved to get a grip on Sasha's expensive suitcase. "A good thing all wives aren't like you."

Chameleon Sasha reverted to the stricken little wife. She was now the colour of alabaster. "I thought you were my friend, Rafe," she said, looking bereft. "You keep sounding more and more like Sandy." Outside the taxi driver beeped his horn. "I have to go," she cried, her breath hissing between her small white teeth. She cast a final frightened look up the staircase, as though the figure of a beautiful woman was leaning over the balustrade. Indeed, for Sasha the whole house was filled with ghosts, moving as one to push her out.

Rafe came back inside a few moments later, pressing his forefingers into his eyes. "Damn!" he groaned. "That woman! I wouldn't be surprised if she refused point blank to enter this house again. She's spooked. I'm not leaving you here on your own either, Alex. It's all too much."

"For us both, Rafe," Alex said. One day she would be able to express her intense gratitude to him. "I'm okay. It's easier now with Sasha gone. This is my home. This is where I grew up."

"Be that as it may, I'm not leaving," Rafe said in a don't-argue-with-me tone of voice. "You can't stay here on your own. First I need to make more phone calls, and then I'll make us something to eat. Mrs. Pidgeon has scuttled off to her sister's place, Sasha very kindly told me."

"I'm not hungry." For once she wasn't about to argue about his staying the night. She wanted to be alone, but not *entirely* alone. Many people drifted in and out of one's life. Rafe was a fixture.

He was looking at her intently. "I don't expect you to be hungry. You've just come face-to-face with a horrible death. Your father's death. But painful as it is, we have to get through it. I'll sleep in the den. You need to rest. We have a long history, Alex. I've always been there for you. I still am."

Anyone would have to call it an unbreakable bond. "You make your phone calls," she said, lifting her chin. "I can make us something light to eat. What would you like?" She knew she could count on a stocked fridge and pantry.

"Anything." Rafe shrugged, his mind on far more pressing matters. It was harvest time for the entire district. Every farm owner would be working flat-out. He had already spoken to Joe Silvagni about getting in as many pickers as he could round up. The bulk of the crop could be picked from the ground. For the rest, picking platforms and poles were available. The harvest was something no one could hold up. Not even the death of Connor Ross.

She could smell the creek, a raging torrent. The spray was kicking up and soaking the bank. As they were approaching "The Rocks," the smooth grey boulders that bulged out of the water, they saw the boulders had turned the racing torrent into a waterfall. The noise of the swiftly moving water was growing louder and louder. It was thrilling. It was incredibly dangerous. Their mother had told them not to go near the leaping tumult. They could watch from a safe distance beneath the eucalyptus trees. Both had promised faithfully they would heed their mother's instructions. No way was Alex going to go anywhere near the edge. The creek, so beautiful, sparkly, and benign for much of the time, was now a tsunami of dirty white foam, clashing currents, carrying broken branches, leaf-stripped boughs, and other debris downstream. A foot or so in front of her Kelvin was mesmerized by the spectacle and hugging his thin frame in excitement.

"Let's go closer, Lexie," he called excitedly.

"No." Her answer was swift and emphatic. She had always considered herself her brother's big sister, not his little sister. She was far more sensible. "Mum told us to stay well back from the water. We promised we would."

Now Kelvin was laughing aloud, his blue eyes sparkling at the thought of adventure. "It'll be okay," He reached out to grab her arm.

"No way!" She pulled back. "The creek has turned into a river. It's dangerous. Look at the way it's smashing over the boulders."

"Why are girls such scaredy cats?" Kelvin teased.

"Not scaredy cats. Girls are more sensible than boys. That's why they don't have as many accidents."

Kelvin punched her lightly on the shoulder. "Then stay here. I won't go far, so you can stop worrying. You really shouldn't be out here anyway. You're just a kid."

"So are you a kid," she reminded him. "Don't go, Kel. Please stay here with me."

Kelvin moved off, unheeding, a gangly fourteen-year-old boy and already a risk taker. It ran through his veins. Kelvin had little sense of caution, while fear gripped Alex like a vise. She desperately wanted to stay where she was. She desperately wanted to keep watch on her brother. The ground that was covered in crushed wildflowers was cold and damp from the heavy spray. Once she fell heavily on her side. Kelvin turned around.

"Okay, Sis?"

"Kelvin, please come back," she begged, rising shakily to her feet. The creek was rushing this way and that with the clashing currents. In the centre, around the jumble of big boulders, it was forming waves. She swallowed and swallowed, her mouth was so dry, and then she began shouting for Kelvin to come back. Even Kelvin, the confirmed daredevil, wouldn't be crazy enough to try to walk across the rocks that normally formed a walkway. Kelvin was exceptionally sure of foot, but anyone would know a boy of fourteen could never survive the rough-and-tumble of the creek, which had turned into a treacherous flash flood. People drowned in flash floods. It wasn't a rare event. It happened all too often.

A shiny black crow flew up from the trees that were branching over her head. Its loud cawing startled her. She looked up. When she looked down, Kelvin, both arms extended for balance, was trying to negotiate the boulders to get to the other side.

She began to run, her heart in her throat, yelling at him to start back. He could just about make it. Instead he kept going, no doubt fancying himself a trapeze artist. She was racing along the bank, calling his name, by now getting herself into real trouble. One slip and a slide and she would be in the water. She was a good swimmer, but no way could she battle a torrent.

"Kelvin! Kelvin!"

And then she saw Rafe. He was coming for her at speed. "Get back, Alex." He almost flung her several feet back onto the thick wet grass. Both of them heard the loud splash. There was no cry from Kelvin. No mad thrashing. To their horror

Kelvin was being rapidly swept away. Lying on her side, the breath knocked out of her, she saw Rafe tearing along the bank with his strong long legs, following Kelvin's downstream path. At one point he must have judged it safe enough to go in, because he dived into the raging waters, intent on grabbing onto Kelvin.

"Please, God. Please, God. Please help them." She followed them as best she could, a roaring in her ears. There would be hell to pay for today. Ahead was a small clearing. As she approached it, slipping and sliding, her heart jumped into her throat. Rafe was pulling Kelvin out of the water.

"Thank God. Thank God." She would thank Him forever.

When she reached them, Rafe was on his knees, bending over her brother's prone body. She saw the blood on Kelvin's head that the torrential waters had not washed away. She was very close to fainting, though she had never fainted in her life. She could see Kelvin's head had been badly bashed by the rocks. Rafe saw it too. He started CPR. He didn't stop until he was forced into the realization it was no use. Kelvin hadn't drowned. It was the serious injuries to his head that had robbed him of life.

She found herself tumbling over Rafe's arched, naked back—his shirt had been stripped from him—a loud pealing in her ears. He turned her twelve-year-old body into his arms, locking them around her. His harsh indrawn breaths were blowing against her wet cheeks.

"God! God! God!" he muttered, over her bent head. He was finding it hard to breathe. Sharp pains were shooting through his chest and shoulders. His legs were bloodied, but nothing broken. He was exhausted, fighting to get enough air into his lungs, yet he continued to hold the weeping, brokenhearted little girl in his arms. Each of them could see into the other's heart. This was a tragedy that would never go away.

Her heart jumped so hard she came awake instantly. "Ohhh!" Her nightmares always came by night. The aura of tonight's nightmare pervaded the darkness. She felt afraid, when she had never felt fear in the house in her life. It had to be the effect of the temazepam. Desperate, she'd taken a couple of her mother's old sleeping pills. They had most probably passed the use-by date. She hadn't bothered to check. She'd wanted to let go. Let it all go.

She rarely took medication, even for a headache. Usually she fell asleep as soon as her head hit the pillow since she worked such long days, but today was different. She needed help to block it all out. At least for a few hours.

It was a gruelling business losing one's father. A child felt love for even a father who clearly didn't love her. She had lived with it even though it had broken her heart. Love for a parent was in the blood. But for her father to go in such a way! Her father had been very proud of his fitness, his physical strength. He could never have endured life in a wheelchair. That would have required tremendous guts, which her father hadn't possessed. Now he was dead virtually by his own hand.

With a concerted effort she got out of bed. As a child she had always had faith her parents would be around. Kelvin too, as a matter of course. All three had died. A whole catalogue of tragedy. She had never had the opportunity to *really* get to know her lovely maternal grandparents, although her mother had taken her and Kelvin on two trips to Ireland before Kelvin died. Her mother had acted as if she were the happiest married woman on earth. She had vivid memories of beautiful, misty green Ireland, a totally different landscape to home, and her grandfather O'Farrell's beautiful estate that had gone to yet another male cousin.

Small wonder she had all but lost her sense of *belonging*. Sadness was something she had always borne in solitude, but a massive sense of desolation was now taking hold of her. Grief had walked the corridors of the house and all the pathways of the estate for years now. Life as they had all known it had changed utterly with the loss of Kelvin. She had never swum in the creek again or painted it in all its moods. The creek was haunted.

Moving in slow motion, she shook her hair out of the thick plait that had come loose, reaching for her robe. What time was it—two, three? She switched on her bedside lamp, looking down at the decorated face of her silver-gilt bedroom clock. Two forty-five.

It wouldn't be the end of the world if she sought Rafe's company. It was a terrible thing to cope with sudden, violent death on one's own. Comfort was what she wanted. Just comfort. She might be hell-bent on protecting her vulnerable heart from Rafe, but she knew she had no stronger or more loyal ally. Her problem was emotional. Psychological trauma. She knew that.

As she made her way silently along the wide corridor, listening all the while, she felt little needles of pure awareness as though someone was walking beside her. Wall sconces made up of scrolling brass branches with glass tulip shades were burning, lighting up the walls that were hung with a collection of botanical prints—orchids, lilies, bromeliads, tropical plants. She had no trouble seeing her way. Rafe had left many of the lights burning downstairs as well. It was *such* a big house. A house built for a big family. A big, loving family.

French doors had to be open because she caught the scent of flowers in the garden, the tropical roses, lilies, the wild irises, frangipani, the blossoming vines that wreathed the house's soaring columns. She drew her robe closer around her body, thinking about what Sasha had said. It *was* a wonder someone, a stranger, not a local certainly, hadn't tried to break into the house. Plenty could be taken that would never be missed. For all she knew, Mrs. Pidgeon could be systematically going off with the silver. Probably not. Sasha would be on to her like a hawk.

Sasha!

She knew in her bones Sasha was going to cause a great deal of trouble. She was hell-bent on it. Sasha was less likely to be agonizing over the premature death of her husband than thinking of ways to make the best of her situation. Sasha had married for money; now she would be set on negotiating the best deal she possibly could as Connor Ross's widow.

There was no point in trying to sleep. The hours passed, his body half numb with shock. God knows how Alex would cope. Sleep was out of the question. His mind was far too active. He got up from the long, comfortable sofa, intending to go to the kitchen to make coffee, but came to a halt as he moved into the entrance hall. Part of him desperately wanted to go up the stairs. To be with Alex.

Discipline, discipline, his inner voice dictated.

He sensed more than heard a sound. He looked up. His throat went suddenly dry. It was Alex floating down the stairs to him. She looked so beautiful, so ethereal, she might have been an apparition. He stood perfectly still, staring in fascination, feeling as if he were moving in and out of reality. Was she truly there, or was she a figment of his overheated imagination? This was such a strange house. A "fantasy house" his mother had always called it.

"Rafe?" His name reached him on a whisper.

"Hello there." He damn nearly stammered, he had been holding his breath so long. "Couldn't you sleep?" It became clear to him Alex needed comfort, another human being to talk to, one she loved whether it was articulated or not.

She drifted farther down the stairs, her face and body illuminated by the light from the wall brackets. The hem of her long nightdress and robe swirled around her feet. The material had the lustre of satin. "I was asleep up until now," she said, giving vent to a sigh that sounded, to his ears, tormented. "I took a couple of Mum's old sleeping pills."

"Wouldn't they be out of date?" he asked, with a quick frown.

"Out of date or not, they worked. At least for a while. The problem was I started to dream. The same old agonizing dream, Rafe. You know the one. You have them too. Where were you going just now?"

"Before I got sidetracked by your apparition, you mean?" He tried for a little controlled humour. "I'd decided to make myself a cup of coffee, since sleep was out of the question."

"Pretty well hopeless on a night like this," she agreed, with a broken little laugh. "Perhaps everything might seem better if we're together?" she suggested. "We can talk."

"Alex, talk is not the answer. What you need is a good long rest."

"Isn't that right!" She had reached the foot of the staircase, holding on to the mahogany finial. "Make your coffee. Include me."

"No, Alex. You don't need coffee."

"Okay, then I'm going to curl up on a sofa in the den. We can... talk... until... dawn." Her words were softly spoken and drawn out. They faded as she moved silently around the big Chinese fish bowl full of luxuriant ferns, heading in the direction of the den.

He didn't bother with coffee. It hadn't been a good idea anyway. He had the feeling Alex would drift back to sleep if she were lying down. The sooner the better. He half closed his eyes, abandoning himself to the strange languor that was filling his body. Alex was right. They went back so far, in times of trouble they needed one another to be no more than an arm's length apart.

The "den" wasn't a den in the usual sense, he had always thought.

It was a large, traditional nineteenth century study. A gentleman's sanctuary. The walls were lined with floor-to-ceiling mahogany bookcases filled with all manner of gilt-tooled, leather-bound books. There was a huge mahogany partners' desk with a green leather writing surface, still set with the beautiful objects Alex's grandfather had favoured. Two antique globes on stands, one terrestrial and the other celestial, stood to one side. He had always admired them. The O'Farrells had been very classy people, but with a considerable talent for fitting in with lesser mortals.

His eyes went immediately to where Alex was lying on one of the velvet upholstered sofas. A sapphire-blue velvet cushion with a gold border was behind her head. Her wealth of glossy blue-black hair was spilling over her shoulder and down her back. All sorts of sensations ignited inside him, flaring fast. He stamped down the flames, thinking he wouldn't get much peace that night. Alex was a maddening woman. But tonight she needed comfort. He took the striped armchair to the right of the marble fireplace that to his knowledge had rarely been used. It was simply part of the decorating scheme. The Old World imposed on the New World.

"You're not going to sit up all night, are you?" she asked him, her voice barely audible. Her mother's sleeping pills had continued with their effect.

"No, but I will wait until you go to sleep."

"Thank you, Rafe." It came with a vulnerable softness she rarely showed. A moment later she said, "There's a very high price to be paid for doing something foolish, isn't there? God, Dad's bleeding head." She put a hand to her throat as though it had been pierced by cold steel.

"Alex, stop." He spoke with firmness. The day had been horrible for them all. The paramedics had been visibly upset. Paramedics had a very tough job. They had been through a similar incident only three months before.

"Come and sit beside me." It was an invitation delivered in a gentle mumble. "There's plenty of room." There was not a trace of seduction in her voice. "If only we could go back to where we were, Rafe. You were my... hero. You..." Her voice trailed off as her arm fell to her side.

"I still am." Incapable of resisting, he rose and went across to where she was lying. She tried to draw herself up, to give him room.

He took control. He half lifted her upper body, settling himself into the corner of the sofa, before pulling her back to rest against him. Immediately her head lolled onto his shoulder as if it were too heavy for her long, graceful neck.

His inner voice came with a strong warning. *Pretend she's twelve again.*

She was beautiful even then. He slid one of his arms lightly across her, his body fighting a war with his mind. "Go to sleep, Alex."

"You're good at taking care of me," she said with a tenderness he had thought gone forever. "I haven't been very kind to you."

"No, you haven't," he agreed.

She sounded baffled. "I don't mean it, you know. I'm so tired of grief."

"Me too." Her pain was his pain. Would the pain never end?

Her voice grew fainter. "Our lives would have been different if Kel... if Kel..."

"Go to sleep, Alex," he repeated, deepening his tone to hypnotic. "Sleep."

She rolled her head slightly to look up into his face, and then she slowly guided one of his hands farther around the soft warmth of her body. The ribbons that tied the neck of her nightgown were unravelling. He could see plainly the upper curves of her small, high breasts, the shadowed cleft between them. How did a man go about freezing hot blood? It all seemed like a bittersweet dream.

"Poor Rafe," she murmured, on a hungering cadence. "Poor Ra... ph... ael."

His full name fell as softly as tears. When she was a little girl she had often called him Raphael to tease him. His name was a nod to his father's first name, Ralph. His heartbeat began to slow. He felt a sudden calm that he hadn't been able to feel for a long time. Despite his certainty he couldn't possibly fall asleep, he did. As if by magic.

It was almost nine o'clock on another blazing blue and gold day before Alex woke up. The French doors were wide open. Scents and sounds were streaming in. She was lying on a sofa in the den. Velvet cushions surrounded her, propping her up.

"Dear God!" The harvest had begun without her. She sat up so suddenly, for a few seconds her head went into a spin. There was no sign of Rafe. Why would there be? Rafe had left her to sleep while he was taking care of business. She needed him, his skills and his dynamic energy and natural authority at this time. Even Joe, her foreman, called Rafe "boss." Joe had never called her father "boss." While her father, may he rest in peace, awaited burial, he would have understood the harvest had to proceed. She couldn't lie about any longer.

She stood up purposefully, rocking slightly on her feet. Unused to medication, her head felt muzzy. A couple of cups of strong coffee would clear it. She could feel Rafe's presence still in the room. She could feel the pressure of his arm around her; the scent of him on her skin. She couldn't ask herself what she was about. Her behaviour had been bewildering to her and to Rafe. She had tried to shut him out. Being Rafe, he knew how to get in. The big question was, had she been punishing Rafe because she had suffered so? So much had been taken from her, it had become very hard to give back.

You always hurt the one closest to you.

Chapter 3

The whole town had turned out for Rose Anne Ross's funeral. Connor's funeral would be different. Alex had decided on a small, private service for her father with only their closest friends, all country people whom she had known all her life. A good friend from her university days, Amy Bateman, had flown in from Brisbane to support her after Alex had e-mailed Amy the sad news. Amy would be staying on for a week, having been granted leave from her law firm, Bateman and Norris, where her father was a senior partner. That certainly helped.

Death in the family brought one face-to-face with funeral arrangements. Alex's father hadn't been a Catholic, indeed he had constantly ridiculed her mother's faith, yet Connor Ross's funeral service was conducted at the same Catholic church where he had been married to Alex's mother, all those years ago.

The full realization she was the only one left of her family fell heavily over Alex. She sat with Rafe, Amy, and two of her mother's closest friends, at the head of the congregation. She had "a little black dress" in her wardrobe—who didn't?—which had to do. Before the service, she had gone in search of a big picture-hat of her mother's. Her mother had always worn wide-brimmed hats to protect her beautiful Irish complexion. The one Alex chose was a soft golden beige with ivory silk roses. It wasn't black, but it looked appropriate and it would keep the hot sun off her face.

Although Rafe had paid Sasha a courtesy visit at the motel where she was staying, Sasha had professed herself far too distraught to attend.

"I just can't do it, Rafe." Sasha, still badly shaken, had showed no change in attitude. "Death has a taint."

Rafe had fully expected her response. All Sasha was worried about were the ramifications for her.

Although she wasn't fully aware of it, Alex spoke beautifully and touchingly not only of her father but also of her mother, as a way of softening her father's image in the town. She did it so well, the small congregation found themselves nodding along with her, tears in their eyes. No one would have claimed Connor Ross had been a wonderful family man, but when it came his turn to give a brief eulogy, Rafe was also generous to his memory.

In sum, no one wished to speak ill of the dead. The melancholy graveside service was conducted by the parish priest at the O'Farrell family plot, where a congregation of stone angels spread their wings. Connor Ross was buried beside his first wife and his son.

The small party of mourners had been invited back to the house for refreshments in the established tradition. To Alex's great surprise, Mrs. Pidgeon had returned to the homestead with no urging from anyone. Tragedy, it seemed, had turned her into a different woman. Gone was the familiar scowl. She could not have been more kind or supportive, saying she would take charge of a buffet for the day.

"Just leave it to me, Ms. Alex."

Alex was greatly relieved. Mrs. Pidgeon hadn't picked up on Sasha's "Sandy" either. She thanked the seemingly miraculously changed woman, grateful for the help. Did one learn compassion from tragedy? It lifted the heart to find one could.

They hadn't been assembled at the house more than an hour when Sasha staged her arrival.

"No doubt she's invigorated, now the funeral is over," Rafe said.

"You have to hand it to her, she's got a lot of gall," Alex said with resignation.

"Gall is essential for gold diggers," Rafe pointed out.

Sasha was accompanied by a tall, well-built man, late fifties, with a whole lot of iron-grey hair and a neatly trimmed moustache and beard. He was impeccably dressed in a summer-weight grey suit, pristine white shirt and black tie, a gesture, one supposed, to the sad occasion. As the two entered the drawing room all conversation abruptly cut out. Older mourners stood, looking blitzed. How could Connor Ross's second wife not attend his funeral, then arrive for the wake?

The very recent widow didn't appear as if she had been privately grieving, too distraught to attend. Indeed she looked dazzling, dressed to the nines. She wore a very smart black suit that showed off her petite figure, a large diamond brooch glittered from a jacket lapel, and a small cluster of diamonds sparkled at her ears. She wore her signature very high heels, the finest black stockings, and an expensive designer handbag that Alex knew had cost a few thousand.

How had she pulled it all together so quickly? Alex wondered, her dominant fears now confirmed. That suit hadn't been bought locally, certainly not the bag and shoes. Alex knew the jewellery had been her father's wedding present to Sasha, no doubt picked out by her in the full flush of excitement.

Amy rushed to her friend's side to stand guard. She had first given Sasha and the man accompanying her a thorough inspection. "Merciful Heavens, Lexie! Is *that* your step-ma? Well! Well! Well! Now isn't she a piece of work?"

"You're being polite."

"It wasn't a good plan, your poor old dad marrying that woman."

"Indeed it wasn't. You know the old saying, marry in haste, repent at leisure." Only her father, not yet fifty, had been neither old nor a fool. He had needed sex, preferably respectable and on call, at that time of life.

Amy laid a hand on Alex's arm. "Can't she bring herself to look a *little* heartbroken? I'm impressed by the suit, but what's with the Marilyn hairdo? She's coming this way, girl."

"No doubt to offer her condolences."

"Just wait until she finds out about the no-show will," said Amy with genuine concern. "This is as bad as it gets. I know the formidable-looking guy with her. He's Todd Healey. He's a lawyer, the expensive, confrontational kind. Time to bring in Rafe, I'd say." Amy's rapport with Rafe had been instant. Alex hadn't for a moment doubted it would be. "He was out on the veranda with the Morrisons the last time I saw him. This is a very awkward situation. I wonder what our merry widow is playing at?"

"I dread to think." Alex's heart was starting to pound. Sasha was perfectly capable of making a scene. Perhaps another time, another place, Sasha might have strutted the boards. She was fast emerging as a suspicious character. A runaway? But from what? Maybe everyone was on the run from something.

"Looks like a time of crisis to me." Amy made her decision. "You'd be shocked at the number of people who skip the all-important business of making a will."

The night before, they had searched the house for more than two hours in a combined effort to find Connor Ross's will. Alex had assumed, up until then, her father's will would be in the hands of the family solicitor, Max Hoffman. When she had inquired, Max had shocked her by telling her Connor had not made his will with him. Max and his wife, Valerie, had joined them in the hunt. No will could be found when they had searched every possible nook and cranny. There was so much paperwork everywhere; a ton of it in the many drawers of her grandfather's partners' desk. She would have to go through it carefully at a later date. Not that her father would ever have left any will there. He had not cared for his wife's distinguished parents.

It was Amy who had voiced the collective opinion. "Looks like your dad died intestate."

Alex found she didn't have any difficulty accepting that. Her father had been completely indifferent to taking care of business.

"I had spoken to your father, Alex, about making a will. Several times in fact," Max had assured her, looking deeply troubled as if the omission were his fault. "He never came to see me. Never asked me here. I couldn't keep persisting."

"No, Max. I understand. You know what Dad was like. He wouldn't have been able to accept he was going to die. Not for a long, long time."

"I'll go get Rafe." Amy's voice brought Alex back to the present. Her good friend Amy was a very attractive young woman with long dark hair, a smooth olive complexion, golden-brown eyes, tall and slim like Alex. She was flushing slightly. Rafe had such a knack for drawing people to him, Alex thought. Amy had been quick to fall under his spell and she was no pushover. Amy, clever and well connected, had more than her fair share of admirers.

Another fraught moment passed while Alex awaited the arrival of Sasha and her lawyer.

"Good afternoon, Sandy." Sasha gave her stepdaughter a fuchsia slash of a smile before introducing Todd Healey, who was regarding Alex keenly out of deep-set grey eyes.

"Please accept my condolences, Ms. Ross," he said in a quite cultured voice, taking longer than necessary to release Alex's hand.

Alex responded with natural-born poise. "Thank you, Mr. Healey. Please, there's tea and coffee," she said, adhering to the courtesies. "Something stronger if you want. The buffet is in the dining room." She gestured off to the left.

"I'd like that," Healey said smoothly.

Sasha looked like she thought Alex should have run everything past her. "I think I know where the dining room is," she said, ready to decline the invitation. "I'm not—"

"Yes, you are," insisted Healey, taking Sasha firmly by the arm. It was obvious he wasn't going to let go.

"Mrs. Ross and I will join you later," he told Alex with a brief smile, clearly referring to the will reading.

Well, he and Mrs. Ross would have to remain in ignorance until then, Alex thought. She was prepared for some unadulterated awfulness from Sasha and a battery of legal questions from Todd Healey. Sasha's arrival had hurried up the departure of the mourners. Alex would be amazed if word of Sasha's turning up at the house with her lawyer in tow wasn't common knowledge around the town before the sun went down.

"If I live to be one hundred, doubtful though that might be, I don't believe I'll see the like of that woman again," a friend of her mother's, indignation writ large on her face, whispered to Alex on her departure. "She wants a good kick up the backside."

Alex wouldn't have minded giving it to her.

Rafe was moving, unhurried, to her side. He was such a pleasure to watch, Alex thought. Rafe was very athletic, very graceful on his feet. Like most of the men, he had removed his tailored black jacket in the heat. The top button of his snow-white shirt was undone, but his silk tie, black with a silver and blue stripe, flowed down his chest. His whole aura was one that would make any woman feel secure.

"Connor's dying a quiet death is looking an impossibility with Sasha and her lawyer around," he said as he joined her. "You didn't say anything?"

She turned her head to him, her voice low. "No. Nothing."

"Good. We have the element of surprise! Everyone has decided to take themselves off."

"They don't want to cause me further embarrassment, and I'm grateful. Dad left a lot of problems behind him, didn't he, Rafe? Sasha is only one of them. We'll need tax office clearance. His personal debts, whatever they are, will have to be paid off. An administrator—"

Rafe turned her slowly to face him, his hands on her shoulders. Even his hands gave off energy and magnetism. "All this can be attended to, Alex. There's no need to confront it today. Handling Sasha will be enough. The lawyer will want to get down to business right away. Amy tells me Healey has a reputation for getting results. No doubt that has made Sasha feel highly optimistic. We have two lawyers of our own on hand, Max and Amy. Later we can hire the experts in their field if we have to. How can Sasha afford this guy anyway?"

Alex made a helpless gesture. "Maybe it's a no win, no fee?"

"No way!" Rafe spoke emphatically as he released her. "Healey will have done his homework. But there's one thing missing he's not aware of. For that matter, neither are we. Sasha's a mystery woman. No friends or old acquaintances have turned up. No family. No ex-lovers. You were the first to recognize this. It might be time to check her out. I could be wrong, but I don't think Sasha is her real name. She still has a trace of a Kiwi accent, have you noticed?"

"I have," Alex said, "but it was something I hadn't given much thought to. New Zealanders are cousins. There's a strong trans-Tasman sense of family. Hundreds of thousands of New Zealanders live in Australia. Probably up to a million."

"Like them, Sasha left. She probably thought she would go further, or she's on the run from something. I wouldn't be in the least surprised. And isn't everyone supposed to go on-line these days?" he asked. "Sasha has no Facebook page, no nothing. No former address that we know of. She's right off the radar. Some might think it difficult in this day and age, but people can and do live their lives in the shadows. Sasha could well be one of them. We're not in any doubt she married Connor because she believed him to be a very rich man. He would have given her that impression just for the hell of it. He was like that. Are you sure there isn't some hidey hole we've missed? That's the trouble with a huge house like this. There are so many places to hide things. So many places to forget where you've hidden them. Places you, Alexandra, mightn't even know about. Your O'Farrell grandad had his quirky side. Is there some secret hidey hole he may have used? On the other hand, Connor could have left his will in some book in the library."

Alex laughed in spite of herself. "Dad had no interest in books, Rafe. He never went into the library any more than he went into my grandfather's study."

"Great! I don't fancy rifling through a million books," he said with a wry half-smile.

"I need to tell you something."

"Fire away." Rafe flashed her a brilliant, questioning glance.

"I can't find my mother's jewellery," she confessed. It was as though the collection had disappeared into thin air.

Rafe shook his head. "Joke, right?" He looked back incredulously. "It's a joke."

"I wish," Alex said. "Only I'm serious. I had thought they were in the boxes in the Italian *cassone* at the end of Mum's bed. Or failing that, on the top shelf of her wardrobe."

Rafe groaned. "Man, I hate to say this, Alex, but you had one dysfunctional family. With all due respect to your parents, neither one of them kept their affairs in order."

"Neither of them knew how." Alex spread her hands helplessly, palms up. "My mother was meant to move into a good marriage, with her parents living somewhere close by. That definitely didn't happen. She was just a girl when she fell madly in love with my father, who thought all his Christmases had come at once. No wonder my grandfather made certain Dad couldn't get his hands on the estate. It was a will that had been very carefully thought out. Lavender Hill was deeded to my mother. With Kelvin gone, the estate would go entirely to me. I really don't want anything from my father. No will or not."

"Hang on." Rafe was making no attempt to conceal his dismay at the turn of events. Connor's death had raked them all. "Whatever your father left after all debts have been paid off would be equally shared by you and Sasha. You don't need me to tell you that. You're—"

"Let me speak, Rafe. As far as I'm concerned, Sasha can have the lot. You know how it goes . . . my worldly possession I thee endow."

"Well I *don't* know. Your father owes you a deep debt of gratitude. You're the one behind the current success of the plantation. Let's sit tight. Wait and see."

"But, Rafe, I didn't do it for Dad," Alex confessed, with a stab of guilt. "Well, not really. I've done it for *family*. The O'Farrells, my mother's family. God knows where my father came from. There's another person of interest."

"I guess you could say that. Connor simply arrived in town one day," Rafe said. "He actually offered his services to my grandfather."

Alex blinked her thick, sooty-black eyelashes. "What?"

"It's true. It's never been mentioned, I know. My family felt no need. Connor wasn't interested in working hard for his money. At least that's the story. He had to move on. Later, he met your mother at some town function or other. He would have been a very handsome young man, with a roguish charm. I imagine your mother fell in love with him on sight."

"She always said she did," Alex answered, unconsciously adopting the same rueful tone her mother had once used. "The honeymoon would have been over fast. My mother was the sort of woman who believed she had made her bed; now she had to lie in it. She had a long list of virtues, but speaking up for herself wasn't one of them. She'd been the adored, overprotected, only daughter of two doting parents."

"Two doting *rich* parents. Your mother never did get to stand on her own two feet. It's the easiest thing in the world to make mistakes when one is young," Rafe said, in defence of the beautiful, gentle Rose Anne he well remembered. "I'd be astonished if Connor left very much at all. He couldn't manage the estate. He never did have a head for business. He unloaded the job onto you, knowing full well you would be able to handle the work. First up, you got rid of Ralston."

"Ralston didn't thank me for that." Alex gave a faint shiver. She had always found Bob Ralston on the creepy side.

"Ralston is a grade-A psycho, or close enough." Rafe looked back at her closely. She was wearing a black dress, simple in style, but it flowed down over her lissom body. She had taken off the wide-brimmed hat he remembered Rose Anne had once worn. Two beautiful O'Farrell women. Alex's long hair was caught up in some sort of high-gloss semicircle around the back of her head. Her dazzling blue eyes and the light application of a deep pink lipstick were the only colour in a face near marble-pale. One way or another, Alex's parents had demanded a high price of their only daughter. "Ralston hasn't approached you, harassed you in any way?" he questioned, his eyes narrowing.

"No, no, Rafe!" Only she was well aware there was bad feeling there. Ralston had first run off the rails when his wife had left him for an itinerant farm worker.

"If he causes you the slightest worry, *tell* me."

She waved her hand vaguely. "He doesn't worry me." She wished had never come up. Rafe had a very protective attitude towards women. Particularly her. "Sasha is the one worrying me. Her behaviour tells us very clearly the thing uppermost in her mind is money. She must have convinced Todd Healey she could pay him for his services because a whole lot of money is coming her way."

"Well, that's her story and she's going to stick with it. You don't have to go through any third degree, Alex. Especially not today. Sasha and her lawyer can arrange their meetings in Max's office. You'll still retain him?"

"Of course." Alex nodded. "Maybe Sasha won't believe us. Maybe she'll accuse me of hiding Dad's will."

"Well, there is a strong chance of that," Rafe said dryly. "Let's wait and see."

They gathered in the library, a perfect place to have a serious discussion. Valerie, Max's wife, had gone home, so there were six people seated around the spacious, book-lined room. A large formal portrait of Alex's grandfather, in oils, stared down at them. His vivid blue eyes appeared to range over everyone in turn, even following them around the room. Alex recalled her father had said the portrait of her O'Farrell grandfather always made him feel like an interloper.

Her nerves were on edge, but she appeared totally calm, in large part because Rafe sat beside her, his expression signalling this was going to be a civilised meeting or it would be shut down. Max kicked off, informing Sasha and her lawyer that, although an intensive search had been made, Connor Ross's will had not been found in the house.

There was total silence; then Sasha, caught completely off guard, exploded. She leapt up from her chair as if she were ready and willing to get into a knock-down, drag-out fight. "I don't *believe* you!" she cried. "It's a f—ing lie. You're making this up."

Old-school Max stopped, startled by her language and her vehemence, unsure how to go on.

Rafe threw up a hand. "Please sit down again, Sasha. No one is making anything up. We've spent hours searching for Connor's will." He wasn't about to tell Sasha and her lawyer the search had only been last night.

"But I was given to understand he had made the will with you, Mr. Hoffman," Healey interjected, glancing sideways at Sasha with a heavy frown.

"I'm afraid he didn't." Max, looking the picture of respectability, shook his head. "I put as much pressure on him as I reasonably could to make a will, but if he did, he never came to me. You can be absolutely certain of that."

Sasha was looking as outraged as any woman could get without physically attacking someone. "Connor told me he had made a will with *you*," she cried as though the louder she said it the more it must be true. "I was his sole beneficiary. Sandy sure wasn't the love of his life. He reckoned she had received far more than her due. He told me—"

Alex, beyond heartbreak, cut Sasha off sharply. "I'd appreciate it, Sasha, if you'd stop calling me Sandy. You do it because you dislike me."

"And you me," Sasha huffed, disconcerted. She turned to her lawyer, who was sitting back, a shrewd eye moving over every member of the group much like a barrister would select a jury. "It's just like I told you, Todd. She hates me."

Rafe raised an eyebrow. "That's utter rubbish! There isn't enough to you, Sasha, *to* hate."

Max broke in quickly. "The purpose of this meeting is to have an informal chat. We were all shocked to confront the fact Connor may had died intestate, although that has yet to be established through more investigation."

"Indeed," Healey agreed smoothly. "We now need to go further afield. If Mr. Ross didn't make a will with you, Mr. Hoffman, he may well have made it with some other law firm in town."

"I doubt it," Rafe said.

"If a will has been made, it will be on record and easily found," Healey countered.

Mrs. Pidgeon chose that moment to enter the library, pushing a trolley that held freshly brewed coffee with a wonderful aroma, fine English bone-china coffee cups, saucers, small plates, and a platter of homemade biscuits.

"Ah, here's coffee," Max said, drawing a relieved breath. He'd never liked the woman Connor had married, but now she seemed to have turned into a fire-breathing dragon right in front of his eyes.

"Who the hell cares about coffee?" Sasha threw up her hands. "We're here for the reading of my husband's will, in which he left everything he had to me. Now you have the effrontery to tell us there *is* no will." Furious, she turned on the housekeeper. "Get out."

To her credit, Mrs. Pidgeon didn't appear intimidated, much less properly chastised.

"Thank you, Mrs. Pidgeon." Alex ignored Sasha, speaking directly to the housekeeper, in a contained voice. "Coffee is welcome. If you'll just wheel the trolley farther in, we can serve ourselves."

"Right you are, Ms. Alex."

"Ms. Alex!" Sasha, a surprisingly good mimic, mocked the housekeeper's country accent. "Don't pay any attention to me, oh no!" Sasha threw up her arms theatrically. "It's all *Ms. Alex* now."

That only caused more aggravation. "And here I was thinking you were a lady, Sasha," Rafe said. "Now it seems like it was all an act. It would be a good idea, however, if you didn't continue to raise your voice. Connor may well have intended you to be his sole beneficiary. I hope his will comes to light this coming week. You are, might I remind you, a guest in Alex's house."

"Only we intend to prove that wrong, Rafe," she cried, as confident as if she were waving a foolproof document aloft.

Healey put out a restraining hand. "My dear Mrs. Ross, it's nowhere near as simple as that." He leaned forward, looking at the others. "You understand, of course, I will be making extensive checks. According to my client, her late husband suffered what she has described as 'a raw deal' in his first marriage."

"How would she know? She wasn't around," Rafe remarked in a sardonic voice.

"I know because he *told* me," Sasha insisted. "The way he was treated upset him greatly. He was treated like chickenshit."

They all winced at the description. The truly bizarre thing was Sasha's Kiwi vowels were becoming more apparent.

"I don't believe my father told you any such thing, Sasha," Alex said, not greatly concerned about Sasha's comments.

"I'm not wrong, I'm damn right!" Sasha burst out. "You should have been there when Connor told me about the way he'd been treated by his wife's parents, those high-and-mighty O'Farrells. The barely hidden contempt—he was nowhere near good enough for their darling daughter—the pressure that was put on him. They hated him, you know, just because their daughter loved him and wanted to stay in Australia with him. His wife made a deathbed will. Connor swore it to me. She made it in a fit of Catholic conscience. Connor told me she didn't want to die with a blot on her conscience."

"That would be extremely difficult for you to prove, Mrs. Ross," Amy butted in, quite shocked, and at a lesser level, entertained, by Sasha's behaviour. "This is all hearsay."

"Who asked *you*?" Sasha was all flushed cheeks and raised voice.

"Might I explain—I'm Amy Bateman, a lawyer as well as Alex's friend," Amy said, succeeding in staring Sasha down.

"Ah, yes, Bateman and Norris." Healey acknowledged Amy with a smile. "I have met your father on any number of occasions, a man who is highly respected, as is the firm of Bateman Norris."

"So what?" Sasha loudly clapped her hands so all attention would snap back to her. "Lawyers are all one big happy family, aren't they?"

"Thanks for reminding us, Mrs. Ross," Healey said.

"Why don't we have coffee," Alex suggested before the situation worsened. Sasha wasn't getting the message at all. Her lawyer didn't like the way she was behaving.

"I'll be mother." Amy stood up, smoothing the skirt of her smart three-piece outfit. Tailored black suit, white silk blouse. Amy looked like what she was: a clever, attractive, confident young woman from a highly respected family.

"Mother be buggered!" Sasha, on the other hand, was giving every appearance of a woman who was quickly losing it. "We're not going to stop until all the wrongs are righted. Connor was entitled to a half share of the estate. He chose not to come forward with his wife's deathbed will because he was afraid the town would lynch him."

Rafe groaned, thrusting his handsome head into his hands. "Get real, Sasha. We don't lynch people around here."

"But they ostra—ostra—"

"'Ostracise' might be the word you're looking for," said Alex.

"I tell you, the will exists!" Sasha appeared genuinely puzzled by Rafe's attitude towards her. "Just as *Connor's* does. This is an outrageous cover-up. You're all trying to protect your precious Alex, but I tell you now, I'm not afraid of you lot." She viewed Rafe with bitter disappointment in her eyes. "I thought you were my friend, Rafe. I thought you'd stand up for me."

Rafe yanked his silk tie a few inches down. "Sasha, the real problem *is* you," he said, his expression severe. "You're carrying things way too far. None of us is in the business of hiding things, much less lying. We stand for the truth. As Connor's widow you have clear entitlements, which Mr. Healey here will have already told you."

"In any case I want nothing from my father's will, Sasha." Alex's blue eyes glittered like jewels. She had only just buried her father, yet his widow was ready for a dogfight. "If one can be found. You are welcome to everything he left."

Healey sat back, almost in good humour. "If, and that's a big *if*, your father did die intestate, Ms. Ross, my client, and you as his only remaining child, would split his estate."

"Connor was *rich!*" Sasha was not about "splitting" anything. "Just how rich, we intend to find out. This wasn't one big happy family, let me tell you. Connor was treated shamefully. I want it put on record his daughter treated him with contempt."

"Brilliant, Sasha," Rafe mocked. "But your one-woman attack on Alex won't work. Alex, on the other hand, has a case—"

Alex reached out to lay a restraining hand on his arm. "Don't, Rafe."

"If you can't behave, Sasha, this meeting is going to end very shortly," Rafe warned, regardless of Alex's plea.

"Mrs. Ross, please allow me to handle this," Todd Healey broke in, aware of the rising tensions in the room and how much his client was disliked. Not that he could blame them. He sat, shoulders hunched, his leonine iron-grey head pushed forward. "The only thing that matters is finding the will, if one exists."

"It's a ticket to half the estate," Sasha snapped. "So watch out! Are you up for a fight, because fight you're going to get. Or"—she screwed up her eyes, staring fixedly at Alex—"you can settle."

"You mean Alex can hand over half the estate and you'll go away?" Rafe asked, with a humourless laugh.

"Rafe, I'm only suggesting it could be the easiest answer," she said, seemingly befuddled by his attitude. Her eyes were darting from Rafe to Alex and back again.

Todd Healey stood up, holding out cards to Alex and Max. "My client might well consider starting with a clean slate."

"A new lawyer, you mean?" For a moment Sasha stood slack jawed, then she shocked them all by bursting into tears. "You're saying you don't want to remain my lawyer, Todd?"

"You appear sure you can handle it all yourself, Mrs. Ross," Todd Healey responded quietly.

"A smart move, I'd call it," said Rafe, looking Healey's way.

"You don't know these people like I do, Todd." Sasha began delving into her expensive handbag for a tissue and then putting it to good use. "I wouldn't put it past our heroic Alexandra to tear up her father's will. He didn't love her. He just needed her to help him run the estate. That's all it was. You *can't* walk away from me, Todd. We need to get hold of the mother's final will."

"I never heard from you it was missing," Healey said.

"I decided not to tell you for the time being," Sasha said, head down. "I needed you on board first."

"A huge mistake." Rafe rose to his feet, addressing the lawyer. "It would take forever to convince Sasha that Connor might have been lying to her. Seeking to impress her would be a better explanation."

"That's not true!" Sasha was flushed with anger. "I thought you'd back me one hundred percent, Rafe."

Rafe shook his handsome head. "Why the hell would I do that?" His voice had a lot of snap in it.

"Because I thought we had something," Sasha cried, all of a sudden looking extremely small and vulnerable.

Rafe swallowed a quick oath. "Like what, Sasha? What did we have?"

"Leave it, Rafe," Alex implored, seeing how he was bristling.

Sasha opened and shut her mouth soundlessly, so Alex took the opportunity to address Todd Healey. "It's not that unusual that my father mightn't have made a will. He was almost fifty, you know, physically very fit. He hated illness. To my father, making a will in the prime of his life would be like signing his own death certificate."

"All solicitors are aware of that mindset," Healey answered, as courteous as his client was outrageous.

"It was nothing like that," Sasha cried, by no stretch of the imagination Connor's grief-stricken widow.

"I think we should take ourselves off, Mrs. Ross." Todd Healey turned to her. "I feel it inappropriate to continue with any discussion, given what I've learned. I will, however, let your solicitor know of further developments, Ms. Ross." The expression on his face seemed to Alex to be ambiguous. "Shall we go?" He stretched out a jacketed arm to Sasha, who was now standing with her mouth turned down like a particularly nasty, petulant child.

"My God, Todd, we came here to have it out," she bitterly remonstrated. "Now you want to go when we haven't talked."

"Not exactly the day for a lot of talk," Rafe commented. He didn't know how much more he could take before he blew up. He knew Alex so well he could see, despite her composed demeanour, she was near the breaking point. The black dress showed up the pallor of her skin and her beautiful sapphire eyes were huge. Only Alex, being Alex, rose to the occasion.

"I'll show you out," she said quietly.

"Bitch!" Sasha hissed, totally unable to keep herself in check.

Rafe waved a hand to cut her off. "You know, Sasha, you're really something else!" There were diamond glints in his dark eyes.

"It's okay, Rafe." Alex swiftly intervened, knowing how fierce he could be when aroused. "I'm going to pretend I didn't hear it."

"You will apologize, yes?" Rafe kept his concentrated gaze on Sasha.

"Only because *you* asked me," said Sasha, her light blue eyes shining at him intensely. Then she left with her lawyer. Alex did not deign to show them out.

"I should be off too," Max Hoffman said, breathing deeply. Sasha's behaviour had shocked and unnerved him. He needed to get home to his beloved Valerie to restore his calm. So far as he was concerned, Connor's second wife was a closet nutter.

"I'll drive you home, Max," Rafe offered. Valerie had taken the car.

Max gave him a grateful smile. "Many thanks, Rafe. A few things

I wanted to discuss with you." Max turned to Alex, giving her a big hug and a kiss on her cheek. "I'll get on to this right away, Alex, so please don't worry."

"I'm not worrying, Max," she quietly assured him. "Except how to keep Sasha at arm's length."

"Good as done," Rafe said.

None of them had bothered with coffee. It had gone cold, just as Alex expected. "Why didn't you tell me your step-ma was such a sweet person?" Amy's intelligent face was agog with interest.

"I've never seen her as bad as that," Alex said. "Underneath it all, I have the feeling she's deeply worried about something."

"Missing out, you mean?" Amy asked. "You didn't tell me she's madly in love with Rafe."

Alex groaned. "She gave herself away, didn't she?" She didn't want to get into it.

"Excruciatingly obvious she's got an almighty crush on him. Healey's no fool. He would have spotted that."

"A blind man would." Alex went to the wall to push a button. "I'll have Mrs. Pidgeon make us fresh coffee."

"Great!" Amy nodded, anxious to get back to what she wanted to say. Her instant attraction to Rafe continued to bloom, and she was seeking information. "How does Rafe feel about that? Though I suppose he's used to getting women all hot and bothered."

"He is indeed," Alex answered.

"He reminds me of that guy in the TV series *Poldark*," said Amy with a dreamy expression on her face.

Alex, who had read some of Winston Graham's books and had seen the televised BBC series *Poldark*, had also noted Rafe's resemblance to the lead actor. "I expect it's the *type*, the dark curling hair, beautiful dark eyes, and the smouldering expression."

"I totally love him," said Amy.

"Who, Rafe or Ross Poldark?"

Amy didn't answer. She blushed instead and gave a voluptuous sigh. "Not that I can blame your step-ma. I suppose you'd be madly in love with Rafe too, Lexie, only you grew up together."

"Yes, we did." Alex's effortless little smile cost her. "Kelvin and I looked on Rafe as our hero. He was the big brother we never had."

Amy brushed her long, dark hair off her shoulders. "You wouldn't mind if I tried to get to know Rafe better?" She looked at her friend questioningly.

I've been waiting for something like this, Alex thought. It had been obvious from the word go Amy had been instantly attracted to Rafe. "Not at all." For all the innumerable long conversations she and Amy had had, Alex had never ever mentioned Rafe as the romantic interest in her life.

Amy blushed under Alex's vivid blue scrutiny. "It's not often I run into an eligible man who has so much to offer. And I'm not talking money."

"I know you're not."

"Right!" Amy responded brightly as though she had been given the all-clear.

An immense sadness descended over Alex. Amy was her long-term friend. She would have to let life sort itself out. Rafe might well find himself attracted to Amy for her many fine qualities. He could give up on Alex and all the baggage she carried. Too many problems beat down on her. Too many for a man to contend with. Rafe needed family to carry on the Rutherford name and tradition. In other words, Rafe needed a suitable wife. Amy would fit the bill. Alex's biggest problem would be if Rafe made a life without her, she knew she would be losing an essential part of herself.

Amy's voice snapped her out of her reflections. "What did your father think when Sasha was batting her eyelashes at Rafe?"

Alex didn't have to consider. "It wouldn't have crossed his mind anything untoward would have gone on there. Not for lack of trying on Sasha's part. She wouldn't have allowed marriage to stop her. My father had great respect for Rafe. With another man it might have been different. I knew my father was aware Sasha had only married him for what she could get. Obviously she thought it was going to be a great deal. Sasha's grasping nature had become increasingly obvious over time. Dad might well have realized he had married the wrong woman. It was a very quick wedding."

"Marry in haste, repent at leisure. In which case, what would have been his next step?"

Alex felt her longing for peace and tranquillity turn to dust. "That's what we have to find out, Amy."

"Maybe it's the reason your father couldn't bring himself to make a will?"

Alex sighed deeply. "He never spoke to me about making his will. Of course I didn't ask."

"No." Amy nibbled her full underlip. "With all due respect, love, you had a dysfunctional family. Rafe has a bit of a short fuse?" She found everything about Rafe Rutherford extraordinarily exciting.

"Only when he's being protective," Alex said after a moment's hesitation.

"Of *you*?" A fleeting touch of anxiety marred Amy's expression.

"We've been through a lot together, Amy."

"Of course you have!" Amy exclaimed, her expression clearing. "I'm sorry, Lexie." She quickly changed the subject. "I don't know if Todd Healey is going to stay with Sasha as her lawyer. She really did show herself in her true colours. What's more, she's obviously misrepresented the situation to him, especially about you. We could all see our Mr. Toddster was very impressed by you."

"Which may or may not change his decision," said Alex. "At least he was able to see for himself Sasha was way too quick off the mark suggesting a conspiracy. Now that I really think back, Dad was acting a bit strangely in his last weeks." That fact had slipped her mind. Now it came back. *Even a bloke like me can fall into a trap.* Her father had said that when he had pretty much forgotten she was there. Had he been referring to his marriage to Sasha?

"Really?" Amy's eyebrows shot up. "Maybe he'd had a big change of heart about wifey. It's not impossible he might have wanted to disinherit her despite Sasha's telling us the complete opposite."

"Only dying intestate assures Sasha will get at least half," Alex said, pointing out what they both already knew. "That's if Dad didn't exclude me for some reason or other. I've never seen any evidence he was particularly bitter about being denied joint ownership of Lavender Hill. He knew where he stood when he married my mother. That was made crystal clear to him. On the other hand, he knew he would be treated with respect. He never wanted for anything. We always lived comfortably—settled, prosperous. We were happy enough. Dad adored Kelvin. Dad was the sort of man who had to have a son. I believe he loved me before it all went terribly wrong. Kelvin's death brought about a great change of heart. Neither of my parents could handle it. The shock was enormous. I haven't handled it all that well myself. Sometimes grief grows instead of diminishing over time. It was that way with my parents. Even Rafe, strong as he is, has found it hard to move on."

Amy very gently rubbed her friend's arm. "You're an absolute marvel, Alex. You have so much strength, determination. Why, Rafe told me you've turned everything around on the plantation. You were among the brightest and the best at university, yet you left to look after your mother. That showed real devotion."

"You'd have done the same for your mother, Amy," Alex said. Amy was part of a very close, loving family ready and willing to offer support. "I'm not saying I won't pick up on my studies again. I will finish my degree. What I really want to get back to is my painting."

"I should think so," Amy said, giving Alex's hand a final pat before releasing it. "You have real talent. Rafe told me he has several of your paintings."

"So he does." Alex's reply was rather distant. Amy and Rafe must have had a long, long chat about her. She wasn't altogether happy about that.

"He said you were extraordinarily good, even as a child," Amy continued, so tuned in to her own thoughts she was missing her friend's responses. "You are so, so lucky to have Rafe as a friend. He knows you so well."

"Maybe too well." Alex's reply was bone dry.

That got Amy's attention. "That bothers you?" She showed her surprise in the widening of her golden-brown eyes.

"In a way. We have a knotty relationship, Amy. All that has gone before, I suppose."

"Maybe so, but there's an intensity of feeling between you that's almost tangible."

Alex looked past Amy's dark, gleaming head. "Maybe it's only clashing temperaments. Rafe and I have a lot of arguments."

"Yet you regard him as a very close friend?"

Amy was clearly waiting on her answer. "I do. When I need him, he's there."

"So he's right for the part of hero then?" Amy looked like she was recording every word.

Alex lightened the intensity of the mood by laughing. "I suppose. Can we get off the subject of Rafe?"

"Sure." Amy put on a smiling face. "To get back to your painting, can't you hire a manager?"

"Did Rafe suggest that?"

"No." A shadow crossed Amy's face. "I admit I asked Rafe a lot of questions. He didn't answer many of them, I have to say. I didn't expect him to really let me in. He hardly knows me."

"But he likes you, Amy," Alex said. "He trusts you as my friend."

Amy looked searchingly into Alex's eyes. "You don't think things between you might change? Perhaps you both—"

"It would never work out." Alex stopped speaking as Mrs. Pidgeon entered the library.

"I wonder if we could have fresh coffee, Mrs. Pidgeon," she requested. "Unfortunately, what we have has gone cold."

"No problem at all, Ms. Alex. It's just so awful what has happened. I can't get over it."

Neither could anyone else.

Chapter 4

Alex woke to the clamour of a thousand tropical birds. They marked their presence, embellishing the atmosphere all over the estate. Automatically her heart lifted. No matter what went wrong in life, nature at its most benign had great healing power.

She pushed aside the light top sheet, rising to her feet. No time to lie there thinking about the endless problems that had to be overcome. There was work to be done.

The lychee harvest was already underway. The clusters of fruit had to be picked by hand, so Rafe asked Joe to round up every available pair of hands to get the red, orange-tinged fruit off the trees as quickly as possible. Picking started at first light and never went past ten o'clock in the morning, when the sun was high in the sky. Picking was never done in the full heat of the day. With her father's shocking, unforeseen death, the need to harvest their main produce, a bumper mango crop, had taken priority. Harvesting the lychees was dangerously overdue. In the mounting heat the crop could be ruined. One late afternoon storm could do a great deal of harm.

When she arrived at the orchard, red berries hanging in great clusters from the shiny green branches, it seemed to her like a scene from the Garden of Eden. It was all so very beautiful. Swarms of brilliantly coloured butterflies were humming and dipping into the flowering lantana.

She was greeted by hellos that rang out on all sides. Such a welcome gave her a great sense of community, of gratitude to its people. School kids, boys and girls between twelve and fourteen, were hard at it picking the clusters that hung closest to the ground. They had taken on the job of pickers for a few hours before they had to wash up to attend school. A school bus would be waiting for them at the gate of the estate, eight forty-five sharp. None had asked for payment. They were glad to pitch in, but payment most definitely would be coming their way. Plus some new piece of technology the schools had need of. Alex made the vow.

Around six thirty Alex saw Amy coming. She was dressed, like Alex, in a t-shirt and shorts, runners on her feet. Alex had given her a wide-brimmed straw hat to protect her olive skin from the golden metallic sun. Amy wore it pulled well down over her eyes.

"Why didn't you wake me?" she called.

"You're here now," Alex said. "Sam," she shouted to a boy in her small army of teenagers, "can you show my friend Amy the ropes?"

"Sure, Alex." Sam dashed up to them, taking Amy by the arm. "Follow me."

"Right, boss!" Amy obeyed, throwing a bright smile at Alex over her shoulder. "I love lychees."

"Don't go eating them. There will be plenty of them at the house." Lychee, mango, and coconut pudding had been hers and Kelvin's favourite dessert as a child. These days she liked to use the delicious fruit in a martini.

For nearly four hours, those pickers that remained on the job stripped the plump red berries from the trees. It was Rafe who called a stop, surprising them all. He had only just arrived as the heat was intensifying.

Alex watched as Amy flew like a bird towards him, her face full of delighted surprise. She saw Rafe say hello, bend his dark head to drop a casual kiss on Amy's cheek. Under different circumstances she would have thought it wonderful if her two great friends, Rafe and Amy, developed a romantic relationship, but some crucial part of her, in such a dreadful muddle, could only feel a piercing jealousy that restricted her breathing. She stood quite still, overcome by a feeling that was utterly new to her. Jealous of Amy? That would never do. Amy was her dear friend. She felt ashamed.

Yet she couldn't get out of her mind that time when Rafe had been provoked into kissing her. Again and again. Both of them staggering, intoxicated, totally off balance. She could still feel his hand sliding down over her breast, his thumb working her supersensitive nipple, causing unstoppable little seizures of sensation. Neither of them had been able to control the flames of desire that burned them up. He had told her he wanted her. She didn't doubt that.

But only in the past year had she felt she was starting to hold it all together. That was her aim, to be a woman in control of her own life. She might admit to herself in private she was hopelessly addicted to Rafe. She dare not admit she was, and always had been, hopelessly in love with him. She had experienced more than her fair share of disasters. What a disaster it would be if she couldn't give Rafe what he wanted and he couldn't give her the certainties in life she craved. Not that anyone could guarantee certainties. But she wanted much, much more of Rafe than she would want of any other man.

Slowly, she started down the grassy track, enclosed by the tall green barricades that had been stripped of their luscious red fruit. She understood perfectly Amy's strong attraction to Rafe. Every woman had a longing to be loved by a special man. Rafe Rutherford was as special as they come.

Rafe turned to greet her, the midmorning sun striking his fine bronzed skin. "What do you say—one more day?" he queried.

She nodded rather brusquely. A bad habit. "That should do it. I can't thank you enough, Rafe, for all you've done."

"Everyone was only too glad to help." He sounded equally brusque. Here were two great friends who had somehow turned into sparring partners. "Anyway, I've come to invite you both to lunch at my place."

Amy's voice had a delighted lilt. "Lovely! I'm so looking forward to seeing it, Rafe." She smiled up into his face. "I've been hoping for a tour."

"And you'll have it." He turned to Alex. "I'll pick you up if you like, Alex. Save your having to drive over. You must be exhausted."

She was over-quick with an apology. "I'd love to come, Rafe, but I'm afraid I have too many things to attend to. If you can wait, why don't we go back to the house?" she suggested. "Amy can shower and change, then you can set off."

Amy hastened to remonstrate. "Oh, do come, Lexie. You badly need a break."

"I'll take one as soon as I can, Amy," Alex promised her. "You've worked hard this morning. You'll thoroughly enjoy seeing the Rutherford estate. It's the pride of the North."

"If you're sure?"

"Your week off is slipping away fast. I want you to get in some enjoyment." In that she couldn't have been more genuine.

When they arrived back at the house, Amy went as fast as her long legs could carry her. "Give me thirty minutes, Rafe," she called, her pleasure and excitement unconcealed.

"Take your time." He sounded indulgent.

Alex felt a thrust of real concern for her friend. "I don't want Amy to get hurt, Rafe," she warned as soon as Amy had disappeared into the house. "I know you can see she's attracted to you."

He spun around, his near-black eyes sparkling. "How about you? How do you feel?" He caught her arm, obliging her to stand still under his brilliant scrutiny.

"I wish you'd stop manhandling me." Unsuccessfully she tried to pull away. "I find a man's physical strength utterly maddening."

"Sorry about that. I *am* a man," he stressed, "and there's nothing I like better than handling you. If you're so concerned about Amy, who I'm sure is well able to look after herself, why aren't you coming with us? It's not as though it's a case of three's a crowd."

She breathed out. "I really do have things to do, Rafe. Every moment is precious."

All of a sudden she looked trapped, hassled. He released her at once, raising an issue that had been playing on his mind. "You know we didn't search Kel's room the other night. We all understood how painful that would be for you."

"Impossible," Alex said, a veil now falling over her expression. "Kel's room is almost exactly as he left it. Tidied up, of course." She gave a sad little smile. "My mother put everything in order. No one goes in there anymore, Rafe. It's a shrine."

"I know," he said in a dark, troubled voice. "I don't agree with shrines. I know Kel wouldn't have wanted that. The people we love and lose have a shrine in our hearts. That does it for me. But are you sure your father didn't often go into his room? We both know of his fierce love for Kelvin."

"It's hell on earth to outlive the one person on earth you truly loved, "Alex lamented. "The gods have no worse punishment than that."

"So we can see Connor spending a lot of time in his son's room," Rafe gravely said. "I can even see him falling asleep on Kelvin's bed. He would get some comfort from it."

"It never did sink in Kel was dead," she said, a lone tear sliding down her cheek.

A man always in charge, Rafe made an agitated gesture with his hand. "Oh, for God's sake!" Tenderly, he reached out and gathered up the teardrop with a finger. "I'm afraid for you, Alex. The last thing your brother would ever have wanted was for you to suffer. He loved you. He even called you his big sister, and he wasn't joking."

"His big sister couldn't help him." She was appalled she couldn't really handle the central tragedy of her life no matter how hard she tried. "His whole life lay before him. He never got a chance. Kel's death cast a shadow over all of us. Me, you, my parents, the whole community. No one will ever forget how brave you were."

"Are you going to hold it against me forever?" Rafe demanded, trying to make sense of all that had since happened between them. "I dived in. You didn't. No little girl could possibly have survived that torrent."

"Yet *you* tried to save Kelvin."

"God Almighty, Alex, are you too proud to accept it? I was almost seventeen. You were twelve. I was a very strong swimmer, as you well know. I did what I had to do. I'm no hero. You began to shut me out from that day. Don't bother denying it. That was the first little break that over the years has turned into a bloody chasm. *I* tried to save Kelvin. *You* couldn't. Is that it? You blame me? You have to tell me." Rafe, almost driven beyond endurance, wanted to shake an answer out of her.

Alex shook her head violently, making her thick braid come loose.

Rafe captured her chin, tilting it so he could see her face. "Is that it, Alex?" he repeated urgently. "You blame me?"

Even his angry, frustrated touch set a match to the kindling. "No use talking about it, Rafe." She refused to meet his eyes.

"Maybe you should consider counselling," he suggested in a voice that in an instant had turned ironic.

"How do you know I haven't had counselling?" she retaliated, her blue eyes on fire. "This is what we do, isn't it, lash out at one another like a couple of trained robots. Let's go in."

He extended a long arm. "Lead the way, *principessa*. I might humbly suggest, if you can bear it, and you clearly don't want me with you, to take a look around Kel's room. You may find something. Since you moved into the Lodge, you would have little idea what your father was doing. You weren't here. You wouldn't know what Sasha was up to, either. Something else I need to tell you. Max and I are taking steps to have Sasha checked out. It's clear she's going to make as much trouble as she can. Your mother's will could be on slippery ground. We see that too often in the courts. And Sasha won't want to go to mediation as a solution because she's after everything she can get. I'm convinced she's had a life elsewhere. We all think New Zealand."

Alex was tempted to push her hand hard against the steely strength of his chest. "Why didn't you tell me before this?" She felt hurt and angry, but he covered her hand with his own, winding his fingers strongly through hers.

"I'm telling you *now*. Haven't you got enough on your plate? Or do you only want what *you* want? I'm expected to rush to your aid for some things and back off for others. You're too damned independent, Alex. It's not working for you."

"Well, it's certainly not working for *you*," she burst out, pulling her hand from his. She could feel the pulse hammering away in her temple. "Damn it." The band that had held her thick glossy braid had snapped, causing her hair to cascade down her back. One long, gleaming, blue-black lock fell forward over her shoulder.

"Leave it," Rafe said. "You know," he said, speculatively, "I wouldn't rule out you're afraid of your own beauty."

"Don't be ridiculous," she snapped. "I am what I am."

"You might be once you break free," he retaliated, matching her tone. Again he took her arm, compelling her towards the shelter of the homestead. "I could do with a cold drink."

"The very *best* I can offer you is a cold beer," she returned with more than a hint of challenge.

"If I were in your shoes, Alex," he told her with gentle menace, "I wouldn't push me too far."

Without quite knowing why, instead of donning her usual indoor gear, capri pants with a variety of cool tops, she settled on a pretty calf-length featherweight maxi that hung from spaghetti straps. The colours were her colours, the fabric printed with a swirl of blue, violet, and lime green enlivened by yellow. Suddenly she felt like she had to wrest back a bit of her femininity. Amy was a very stylish dresser, as Alex once had been. Both of them tall and very slim, they made their dresses look good.

After a bit of a hunt she found a pair of silver sandals to complete the outfit. Her hair she had arranged in a loose knot on her nape. She even went so far as to apply a light makeup, she felt in such need of looking something of her old self.

She stood back from the mirrored wardrobe, motionless, lost in sad and complex thoughts. Rafe wanted her to search her dead brother's room. She thought it would be all she could do to open the door. Rafe, as usual, was probably right about her father seeking comfort in his adored son's room. All that had happened twelve years before, when the swollen creek had taken Kelvin, was almost as much alive in their minds as that calamitous afternoon.

While her mother was alive, fresh flowers had always been placed in Kelvin's room. Alex had always done everything for her mother, wishing only to remain loyal to the mother who loved her, but she couldn't remember any instructions that had ever been given to put fresh flowers in *Ms. Alex's* bedroom. Not that she couldn't do it herself. In fact she had. Lavender Hill was a wonderful landscape of fruit and flowers. In a week or so the jacarandas that gave the estate its name would break out in their heavenly lilac blossoms. One had to seize the days of their glory. As November lengthened into December, the monsoon would blow in, raining down hailstones, sometimes so big it was hard to believe, the high winds stripping the jacarandas of their fairy-tale flowers so the spent blossoms formed sodden, outward-spiralling circles.

She stood, head bowed, before the door to her brother's room. She could hear her heart going *boom boom boom*, thudding drumlike in her ears. Rafe had been prepared to lay down his life to save his young friend. She had run along the bank sobbing in an agony of fear. Had that terrible tragedy twisted her soul? Had she really used Rafe to protect her from herself? Had guilt over Kelvin's death made her what she was? One day very soon she would have to sort through her tangled feelings. She put out her hand and opened the door.

Slowly, reverently, she moved into the room, her eyes touching first on the little shrine her Catholic mother had arranged. A statue of the Blessed Virgin, mother-of-pearl rosary beads hanging around her neck. Small silver-framed photos of a beaming Kelvin arranged around it. On one wall his school sporting trophies, a surprising many, were on display. Both she and Kelvin had been athletic. His spick-and-span sports blazer that had been dry cleaned hung outside the wardrobe door. His collection of model Battle of Britain Spitfires and the much later jets hung from the ceiling. There were two big posters of champion footballers on the end wall, and a bundle of his excellent school reports tied with a shining blue ribbon on his desk, which was crammed with family snapshots. His books and his broad range of comics were neatly stacked; the adventures of *Tintin in America* on top.

The bed was fully made up. She moved closer, smoothing the depression caused by a man's large, heavy body lying on top of the mattress. Of course their father had come in here often. Oh God, to be thus! A child taken long before his father. "Dad came in here, didn't he?" she said. "How many times, I wonder? Over and over. Poor Dad."

It was almost as if she could hear her brother's voice. *It doesn't matter now, Lexie. It's over. Please don't continue to mourn. Remember me with love. We'll all be back together one day.*

"It's hard, Kelvin. So hard. The pain! I *failed*."

You didn't fail, Lexie. You were only twelve. You weren't strong enough.

With those words, Lexie felt a dreamlike peace enter her soul. Kelvin was gone, but she could feel him with her still.

It was the mauve prelude before dusk when Rafe brought Amy home. Alex had walked out onto the wide veranda, with its morning glory–wreathed white pillars, to greet them.

Amy, looking like she had enjoyed an idyllic day, ran up the short flight of stone steps to fling an arm around her friend. "Everything okay, love?"

"Fine." Alex smiled affectionately, returning the hug. "I can see you've had a lovely time."

"Fabulous!" Amy enthused. "Rafe ran me around the entire estate. He invited friends to lunch. A lovely couple. We got on extremely well. They were so disappointed you couldn't make it. They missed you."

"Oh?" Alex looked towards Rafe, who had joined them.

"Jon and Miranda," he said, clueing Alex in before she could ask. "They were really sorry you weren't able to join us, but naturally they understood."

"A lovely couple!" Amy said again, pronouncing judgment on lifelong friends. Rafe had been Jonathon's best man. Alex had been chosen by Miranda as her chief bridesmaid, only the plan had fallen through due to the death of Alex's mother. "I'll just run up to my room," Amy said. "Put my things down. I have a big bag of macadamias here."

"The best in the world," said Rafe.

Amy, with a peal of laughter, ran off into the house. Her face had caught a little of the tropical sun, giving her skin the sheen of gold. No other word to describe it: Amy looked radiant.

"Are you coming in?" Alex asked.

"Of course. I want to know what's been happening."

His eyes were moving over her in such a way, she tensed up. She even wished she had thrown on her t-shirt and loose-fitting capris. Those brilliant dark eyes of his had a more than magnetic pull. "Good to see you in a dress," he remarked.

"I needed to feel more like my old self," she said defensively.

"Shall we go in?"

"Did you manage to make a search of Kel's room?" he asked, walking tall beside her. "Tell me before Amy gets back."

She glanced up at him briefly. "I did go in. I felt Kel's presence. I wasn't in the least frightened. I could almost hear his voice in my mind, telling me he was happy, to stop mourning, that we'd all be together again."

Rafe caught her hand, clasping it strongly. "That took guts."

"Dad has been in there many times," she said, allowing herself the brief comfort of his hand. "There was a depression in the bed. I lay down there myself. I felt calm, but I couldn't make a search, Rafe. Not then."

"That's okay. I hope you truly believe Kel is happy. Look at me, Alex."

She lifted her head. "I'm going to tell myself that every day."

"Good girl."

His smile twisted her heart. It would twist any woman's heart. "I'm not a girl, Rafe. I'm a woman."

"Don't I know that better than anybody?" He surprised her by lifting her hand and raising it to his lips.

Little sparkles like firecrackers went off in her chest. Her connection to Rafe was almost primeval; unreasoning, instinctive in a way she could do nothing but accept.

* * *

Amy, skipping lightheartedly down the grand staircase, caught sight of them out on the veranda. That was the moment she let go of her chances with Rafe Rutherford. In a single instant, her whole perspective flipped. They were standing very still, facing each other. Rafe was holding Alex's hand. Both were motionless, yet it seemed to Amy to be an extraordinary display of emotion. A little sigh was torn from her lips. She knew now she had been incredibly naive. She had grasped that the relationship between Alex and Rafe, going back to childhood, was complex. Alex had suffered many traumas throughout her life. They must have taken her down many labyrinthine byways always closed off by Rafe. He was part of everything. Amy found herself muttering a prayer of thanks that her strong attraction was only in its infancy. Whatever Rafe and Alex were to each other, one thing was clear: The bond was way too deep for another woman to break.

The following afternoon Max Hoffman called at the house. Amy, knowing Max was coming, had taken the opportunity to do a little shopping in the town centre. The many variety shops had always attracted the tourists. Alex had lent her the Mercedes, which had once been her mother's and was now hers. It was years old, but it had always been beautifully maintained.

Max gave Alex his wide, friendly smile as he came up the steps to join her. "I passed your friend Amy on the road. She had me fooled for a moment," he said with a laugh. "With her big dark sunglasses and her long hair pulled back, for a minute I thought it was you heading into town."

"No, I'm here for you, Max," Alex said, thinking she and Amy did share a resemblance. Height, build, long dark hair. "Come on in. What is it you have to tell me?"

"It will shock you, Alex," Max warned. "It shocked me."

"Really?" Alex felt her stomach contract. "It has some bearing on the missing will?"

"In a way. Our wily friend Healey called me first thing this morning."

"Let's go into the study," she said as they entered the house. "Can I offer you something, Max? Tea, coffee, a cold drink?"

"Tea would be lovely. I find it very refreshing even in the heat. I can't say the same for coffee."

"Then go on through. I'll have a word with Mrs. Pidgeon."

Max raised his eyebrows. "She's staying on, then?" They had all known about Sasha's housekeeper, who didn't live up to her name. His wife, Valerie, had labelled Mrs. Pidgeon the classic battle-axe.

Alex whispered behind her hand. "She's had a miraculous sea change. We get on very well these days."

"Thank God for that," said Max. "You need all the help you can get."

They were seated at either side of the broad mahogany partners' desk in her grandfather's study. A courteous Mrs. Pidgeon had come and gone, leaving the welcome trolley.

Max took a few grateful sips of his tea before he gave Alex his news. "It appears your father consulted a divorce lawyer in Brisbane, would you believe? That was late August, the twenty-fifth, to be precise."

Alex gasped out loud. "Dad went to a divorce lawyer?" She could scarcely believe it. "Was the marriage as bad as that?"

"Would you actually *know*, Alex?" Max asked, letting his glasses slip down his nose. "You've been living at the Lodge, apart from your father and Sasha."

"Even so, Max." Alex took a long sip of her tea to gain time. "Sasha has never stopped carrying on like the lady of the manor. She didn't give me the slightest hint there was anything wrong with the marriage, rather the reverse. She was claiming Dad would do everything she asked. Even go off and live in the south of France."

"She didn't know your father, did she?" Max smiled wryly. "I don't want to bring up the old tragedy—we all know you've suffered enough—but Kelvin's death brought both your parents to the brink of madness. After your mother's death, some passing notion must have made Connor believe a good-looking, much younger woman could bring him some comfort."

"Never Sasha." There was condemnation in Alex's voice. "Sasha is motivated by greed. I'm sure Dad knew that. He was no fool. He must have found out something about her, or she may have said something that set him off. Rafe told me you're having her investigated?"

"We have to, Alex. That's part of the process. Sasha is no grieving widow. She saw your father as a ticket to wealth. This tragedy, she would think, has put a fortune in her hands. Healey is a topflight lawyer. He wouldn't be representing Sasha if he didn't think it well worth his while. I believe he's going to go after a substantial settlement for Sasha. Certainly enough to keep her in comfort for the rest of her life."

Alex felt dazed. "For the rest of her life?" She stared across the desk, with the old Irish saying: och ocon, "Woe is me," uppermost in her mind. "My family has to be cursed."

Max well understood her reasoning. Of the family—husband, wife, and two children—only Alex was left. "They could claim Connor had been treated unfairly in your mother's will," he felt compelled to tell her. "They could claim your father was the breadwinner while your mother looked after the house, although you always did have a housekeeper who arrived at nine and left at five. Your mother was frail for a long time." *Frail* was the chosen term. Rose Anne's drinking was never mentioned. "They could claim Connor had a lot on his hands. Claim he was extremely helpful. He did everything for her. That she loved him. You would be represented as the daughter who exerted too much influence, turning your mother against your father for your own gain. No will is foolproof these days. Disputes over wills take up a lot of the court's time. Healey could claim a fifty-fifty split of the estate."

"God no!" Her protest came out louder than she intended. "That will never happen."

Max was quiet for a moment. "I've done a quick evaluation of the estate, Alex. It's worth millions. I'll get you a precise figure. Your father wouldn't have had much in the way of personal debt at the time of his death. For once he seemed to have been getting his affairs in order, though it's due to you directly that the plantation is operating successfully. You've turned things around."

"The estate was founded by O'Farrells."

"Of course. The whole town can attest to that. But your mother chose to marry Connor. She didn't exactly defy her parents, but she chose him over a life with them in Ireland. Your mother wasn't a strong woman like you, Alex. And tragically she was terribly reduced by Kelvin's death. Do you think there's *any* possibility there's a grain of truth in what Sasha told you about a deathbed will?"

Her knowledge of her mother's beliefs and sense of duty won out. "Sasha is lying, Max. I'm certain of that. My mother may have been madly in love with my father at the beginning, but I don't think that lasted longer than the honeymoon. In marrying my mother, my father gained the status he craved. And she was very beautiful. She gave him two children. Even before we lost Kelvin there was no real rapport between my mother and father. Dad had worn my mother down. He was actually the last man in the world for her. She would still be alive had she gone to Ireland with her parents."

"And you wouldn't be here, Alexandra," Max gently pointed out. "But we have to consider this. Your parents were married for almost twenty-two years, during which they lived under the same roof. They had two children together. There was never any suggestion Connor had treated your mother badly. He wasn't a violent man. There was no history of abuse. No history of infidelity on his part. To all appearances the Ross family lived a secure, prosperous life."

"Thanks to my mother. You sound concerned, Max."

"There is *some* cause for concern. Healey is very good. But we won't go too far ahead."

"Where there's money, there's always conflict," Alex lamented. "My mother left Dad very well off, as you know."

"Certainly. But Connor was denied part ownership of the estate," Max stressed. "Your mother upheld her father's wishes, leaving the estate to you with the stipulation your father could remain in the house if he so chose, until his death. She wasn't going to toss him out. Not her husband. She had taken him on for better or worse."

Alex nodded. "Dad and I rubbed along okay until he showed up with his new wife. How could I live here after Dad married Sasha?"

"It's a huge house," Max pointed out quietly. "You could have come and gone without seeing anyone."

Alex sighed. "Max, with Sasha being the woman she is, my staying on in the house was untenable. She must have managed to get Dad on her side, because he never said a word to me."

"Maybe she told him you wanted out," he guessed—correctly, as it happened.

Alex considered. "I suppose she could have. She's a born liar and a troublemaker. She took a good look over the Lodge almost as soon as she arrived. She would have realized at once it was a ready-made home for me."

"Obviously she's a woman who works to her own agenda."

"And you think Healey is going to contest all this?" She watched Max's face as he agonized.

"He'll have a good try, Alex. Take George Crowley." He named a deceased multimillionaire whose affairs had been making national news. "His mistress managed to get ten million from the family estate. The family and their lawyers said it couldn't happen, but it did."

"She told a great story in court," Alex said.

"As could Sasha. Tutored, the blond hair brushed out and arranged closer to her head, dressed very differently, she could appear sympathetic to the court. Rafe believes she's playacting all the time."

"He's right about that." Alex dropped her head despondently. "My mother, far from keeping my father short, propped him up. You know that, Max. Rafe knows. The whole town knows. Dad drove the estate heavily into debt. My mother's money bailed him out. Time after time."

"Sasha will claim your father told her a very different story, where he was made to feel humiliated by his wife's financial clout and her handouts. At the moment, Sasha is juggling as many balls as she can in the air. When she finds out—she probably already knows—your father had been consulting a top divorce lawyer, it will take the wind out of her sails."

Alex cheered up a bit. "I do remember Dad taking a trip to Sydney late in August. Sasha didn't go with him."

"I'm not surprised."

"What was the name of the legal firm?" Alex asked.

"Millar and Winterstein. An admirable choice when one is looking for the best divorce lawyers."

Alex couldn't help a wry laugh. "Maybe your PI will turn up Sasha's lengthy criminal record."

"We do think at some stage she changed her name."

"I think we've all arrived at the same conclusion. She wasn't born a Sasha. I've noticed many times she can be very slow to respond when that name is called. At some point in her life she may have thought a more exotic name would work for her."

"We have the best man on the job, Alex," Max said. "It may take a little time, but we will get to the bottom of who Sasha is, not that it's any crime to change one's name. She does have a Kiwi accent. Just a word here and there. We've all picked up on it. So New Zealand born and bred then? I want you to cast your mind back to anything, any criticism however slight, your father might have made of Sasha. Some chance remark about her previous life. A bimbo—I'm sorry—

" Max reddened. "A woman like that would surely have had a man in her life."

"I'd make that *men*. Dad did mutter once in my presence 'even a bloke like me can make a mistake.'"

"Who or what was he referring to?"

"I'm sorry, Max, I don't know. It would have done no good to ask. Dad wouldn't allow Sasha to change anything in the house though. She had all the decorating plans under the sun, but he gave her the thumbs-down before I did. You're right, I didn't often see them together, their interaction, but Dad didn't act at any time like a man head over heels in love with his new bride. Sasha was a toy. Just like my poor mother was. The only person Dad ever truly loved was Kelvin. Kelvin was his world."

Sighing heavily, Max began to gather up his sheaf of financial papers. "Then think how he missed out on his beautiful daughter, Alex. I must get going. I have a late afternoon appointment. We'll move ahead on this, rest assured. Meanwhile you could keep up the search for any will. People hide things in the weirdest places. I have clients who forget where they put things from one hour to the next."

"There's still Kelvin's room," Alex said. "The one place we didn't search."

Max gave her a deeply sympathetic look. "I understand no one goes in there."

"Dad did," Alex answered simply. "I did yesterday, but I couldn't bring myself to search."

"Of course you couldn't," Max said. "Is it possible you'd let Rafe look around? Kelvin thought the world of him. For that matter, so did Connor."

Alex forced herself to keep her voice level, trying her best not to allow tears to spring to her eyes. "I'll think about it, Max."

Chapter 5

Amy hadn't returned from the town by late afternoon. Alex didn't start to worry until it was approaching dusk. Amy had learned the tropical night had a way of coming down like a curtain after the first act. Then too, Amy wasn't familiar with the Mercedes. She would need a moment or two to check how the lights worked, the high and low beams. Alex had thought Amy would be home well before dark.

Time wore on. She tried to shrug off her concerns. It was difficult to imagine Amy getting into any sort of trouble. Amy knew how to look after herself. Besides, there were many variety shops in Endeavour to visit. One sold exquisite silks, hand painted by local artists. Then there was the highly regarded art gallery showing the works of nationally acclaimed artists living in this glorious part of the world with its close proximity to the Daintree Rainforest and the Great Barrier Reef's many islands and cays. She had even managed to get two of her most recent watercolours hung there.

She stayed out in the cool of the colonnaded porch, trying to relax in the comfortable white wicker planter's chair. Any minute, she told herself, she would see the Mercedes sweep up the drive.

It was the sight of Rafe's Range Rover that had her jumping to her feet. She knew Rafe had been out of town on business for the day. She had spotted the helicopter that had taken him to wherever he wanted to go around nine o'clock, yet here he was at Lavender Hill.

The driver's door of the Range Rover was flung open and Rafe appeared. She was quick to see he was disturbed about something. His expression was decidedly dark and edgy. She heard his mobile ring. He stopped to answer it.

She ran down the steps, making a beeline for him. "What is it?" It was clear there was something wrong.

He took her arm, steering her back to the house. "There's been an accident. It's Amy. Before you go into a panic, she's okay. She's been taken to hospital. Edna Mitchell was walking her dog when she spotted the Merc. It had run off the road, half tipped on its side. She was terrified it was you. She ran to it and looked inside, saw it wasn't you. She rang the ambulance and the police. It was a miracle the car didn't roll. The only thing that stopped it was a thick grove of scrub and a few saplings." He exhaled deeply. "I'd just arrived back in town to hear *you* had been involved in an accident. It took a few minutes to double check." Rafe didn't look at her as he spoke. The shock he had received had been enormous. Now he had to remain focused.

A feeling of guilt and anxiety hit Alex hard. Amy was her friend and her guest. For this to have happened! "I lent Amy the Merc," she said wretchedly. "Max was coming, so she decided to do some shopping. She was on her way home?"

"Yes. She was ten minutes away from the estate."

"We have to get to the hospital."

"Of course. That's why I'm here. That was an update I took just now. Nothing life threatening, thank God. Shut the house up and we'll go."

Amy was lying, very pale and very still, in the hospital bed, her hands resting outside the white coverlet. She had been put into a room on her own. A nurse was attending her and smiled at both of them as they entered, but cautioned, "A few minutes only. Our patient needs peace and quiet. She's a lucky girl! She should buy a lottery ticket. No broken bones, just the big bump on the forehead, as you can see. Some bruising. A few scratches. Doctor wants her kept overnight for observation."

"I can *hear* you," Amy piped up in a feeble voice, quite different to her normal confident tones.

The nurse left the room.

"Oh, Amy, Amy." Alex went to her friend, her heart full of regret for what had happened. Gently she took Amy's hand, holding on to it. "I am so sorry this had to happen. But you're going to be fine. You're such a good driver. What went wrong?"

Amy's eyelids drooped as though they were a terrible weight. "I don't know. I don't really know, Alex. One minute everything was okay. I'd had a lovely time shopping. I bought the most beautiful lengths of silk, for you, me, and Mother. I was almost home. The next thing a vehicle came out of nowhere. I swear it hadn't been following me any distance at all. I would have seen it. The road had been empty. It was moving at top speed. I tried to move as far as I could to the right to allow it to pass, but even then, it sideswiped me. I can't really remember what happened next, although I do remember an elderly lady calling out to me. I think she thought I was you, Alex. My head was reeling."

"Of course it was," Alex said tenderly.

"You didn't see the driver, Amy? Man or woman?" Rafe asked for both of them.

Amy turned her dark head on the pillow. "Hello, Rafe." She smiled.

"Hello, Amy." He moved closer to look down at her. "We're devastated this has happened to you. You're very important to us."

Amy got to smile again.

The odd thing about attraction, Alex thought, was it would never go away.

"The make of car, the colour?" Rafe persisted gently.

"The police asked me before the doctor shooed them away," Amy said, looking and sounding very woozy.

Amy's nurse, a big woman, glided silently into the room. "Just like I'm about to shoo you two away, Mr. Rutherford," she lightly scolded.

"Seems we to have to go, Amy, love. I want you home tomorrow." Alex bent to kiss her friend's pale cheek. "I'll ring your family as soon as I get home."

Amy tried to lift a hand, let it drop. "Don't, Alex. Don't worry them."

"Amy, I'm duty bound to tell your mother and father," Alex said. "They must know."

Amy managed a wan smile. "I'm trying to spare you. Ring and you'll have Mum on your doorstep tomorrow," she warned.

"And we'll greet her," Alex said with conviction, although she wasn't looking forward to making that call to Amy's formidable mother, Barbara. Amy had three older brothers, all lawyers, and Amy was the precious daughter of the family.

"If your mother feels she needs to come, we'll look after her,"

Rafe said. "What you have to do, Amy, is make a swift recovery. We'll find the lunatic who sideswiped you."

"I don't think it was an accident, Rafe. He did it deliberately. At lease I think it was a he. A woman, I'm sure, would have stopped. I get the feeling the driver knows Alex," said the sharp-witted Amy.

Alex exhaled a long breath. "You're not to worry about anything," she said, turning at the door to face her friend. "Do you need anything at all?"

The nurse answered for her patient. "She needs rest, Ms. Ross. Don't *you* worry, we'll look after her."

"Then she's in good hands," said Rafe.

They were no sooner in the Range Rover when Alex threw Rafe an agitated look. "Go on, say it!"

"How do you want me to respond to that?" Rafe tightened his grip on the wheel.

"I don't know what life is anymore. Is it Armageddon, or what?"

"If it is, the Big Guy up there is on your side." Rafe's answer was wry.

"Whoever it was who ran Amy off the road, they thought it was me driving the Merc."

"Of course they did," he confirmed. There was no point in ignoring it.

"Why wouldn't they?" Alex cried. "Everyone knows the car. They know the personalised number plate. Who would want to push me off the road? Amy could have been badly injured or killed. It was either criminal negligence, texting someone while driving, or a premeditated attack. All criminal in my book. No one I know drives like a maniac down a narrow country road. Everyone knows where the road leads."

"To the estate," said Rafe. "The police are on to it, Alex. They'll catch whoever it was. Your guess?" He shot her a piercing glance.

"Is there a possibility it could have been a random thing?" she asked with no real expectation it had been. "I suppose we should consider it. The driver freaked out, a lot of people do, went into a panic, turned around, and went back the way he came."

"He or *she* came," Rafe amended. "Whoever it was, they'll be found. I don't think we need worry about that."

"Wasn't it a fool thing to do?" Alex asked, looking sideways at him. "Who hates me enough to try to injure me? Any halfway decent person would have stopped. I suppose it was a further miracle Mrs. Mitchell was walking her dog. A few tourists do take a drive to the estate, but they're not allowed in unless they make a special request." She shook her head as if to clear it. "Would Sasha be crazy enough to try to deliberately run me off the road?"

"Need I answer that?" Rafe asked. "I did have her briefly in mind. Sasha is just loopy enough, I suppose, to try anything if she knew she could get away with it. Fairly difficult if one is driving a late model, bright red Mercedes coupe. The police will take a good look at it as a matter of course, but they're not going to find anything. It's not in her interests to have the police on her back."

Alex twisted to look at him. "Plus the fact that Amy, even in a panic with a car zooming at her, would have noted the other car was bright red."

"Obviously it wasn't *Sasha's* car," Rafe said. "I agree she's incredibly greedy, but she's not a complete fool. Who else is there? No one in the town would harm a hair on your head. If it had been a genuine accident, the driver would have stopped."

Alex felt her nerves spasm. "You don't think it could have been Ralston?" she asked after a moment. "He was very angry I sacked him. I believe he found it hard to get another job."

"He did indeed." Rafe had been keeping a close eye on Ralston. "He's not the most savoury character in the world, but again, he's not a fool. He would know his vehicle would be certain to be checked. Whatever vehicle it was, it would have the Mercedes's paint on it. Even if it were hastily removed, forensics would find some trace somewhere. Ralston could have been in town, caught sight of Amy, and thinking she was you, decided in a mad moment to follow. Anything could have been going on in his head."

"You mean he intended to give me a fright? We know his vehicle. It's a Toyota Hilux ute. He's had it for years. You wouldn't know what the original colour was for the thick coating of dust. I don't think he has cleaned it since he bought it. I think it's dark blue or navy. The Mercedes is silver, so paint flakes would show."

"Whoever it was," Rafe said grimly, "they haven't got safely away."

"Where is the Mercedes anyway?" Alex asked belatedly. Cars could be replaced. People couldn't.

"It would have been towed away. The police will handle it, Alex. They're already on the job."

When he looked in the bathroom mirror, a red-eyed lunatic stared back at him. God, he looked crook! He couldn't quit drinking, no matter what. Drink these days was his only solace since the bloody wife took off with some itinerant guy called Barry something or other. In a way he was glad the guy had taken Cheryl off his hands, but he hadn't counted on the loneliness, much less having to make his own meals. There were stacks of pizza boxes lying about the place.

That afternoon he'd been drinking in the pub. He'd walked into town. He would walk home. He had let everyone in the pub know in case some bastard decided to dob him into the police for driving over the limit. "The ute's buggered!" he'd told everyone at the bar.

The ute had indeed packed it in and he didn't have the money for repairs. He already owed Jimmy Hughes at the garage eighty-six dollars. It was when he was staggering back home in the humid heat, his navy baseball cap pulled well down over his eyes, when he suddenly thought of his on-and-off-again mate, Charlie Wilson. Charlie was away on a week's fishing trip. They hadn't asked him to go, like they used to. He had long since fallen out of favour. Well, since he had lost his job because of that uppity bitch. But Charlie wouldn't mind if he borrowed his old ute for a few days. It wasn't as though Charlie hadn't lent him the ute before when his own was out of action. Charlie's ute, an old spare, was almost as battered as his own, but at least it worked. He knew where Charlie left the keys. Charlie wouldn't mind.

Or so he kept telling himself when he drove his old mate's workhorse out of the carport.

He had almost reached the end of the track that led from Charlie's onto the main road when he spotted a silver Mercedes gliding smoothly along. He had the sensation of a whirring in his head. SHE was at the wheel. Miss High and Mighty, bloody Alexandra Ross. He wanted to scream abuse. He sputtered it to himself, deciding in a split second not to head back to his house but follow the bitch who had sacked him, when her dad *had assured him he would have a word with her and all would be okay. Connor Ross had always supported him. It had upset him to hear poor old Connor had kicked the bucket when he came off his quad bike. A rash bugger, poor old Connor had been. He wasn't fond of quad bikes himself. Too easy to tip over.*

The feeling of depression that had come over him on the way home gave way to an uncontrollable urge to give Miss High and Mighty a fright. Why not? Who did she think she was, anyway? The road behind him and in front was empty of any traffic. It was late afternoon. He sniggered to himself. She wouldn't recognise Charlie's old ute. It was covered in a thick layer of red dust just to add to the camouflage.

He put his foot down hard on the accelerator, hurtling at the shining silver Mercedes. He didn't want to hit the rear of her vehicle full-on; the plan was to sideswipe the Mercedes, forcing her off the road. That would be enough to give her the good shake-up she so richly deserved.

He saw her fight for control, the wheels fighting for purchase on the grassy verge after Charlie's ute slammed into the Merc. He heard the sound of metal on metal. Afterwards, mission accomplished, the Merc tipped halfway on its side, he whipped back into control. He had to get out of there. He spun the ute around, tearing off in the opposite direction.

He had to get Charlie's ute back home without being seen. Any signs of damage he could clean off before throwing a can of soil back on the area. He wasn't angry and frustrated now. He felt good. No witnesses to what had happened, either. When the coast was clear, he would cut back across the fields to his home. He might even pour himself a Jack Daniel's to go with his cig. When the cops checked him out either at the pub or the house, he was in the clear. When Charlie came back from his fishing trip he wouldn't even bother looking at the ute. It was practically a bloomin' write-off anyway.

If it had been heartbreaking for Alex to enter her dead brother's bedroom, Rafe found it was hard for him as well. He had never spoken of the agonies he had endured for years after Kelvin's death. The nightmare of dragging Kelvin's body out of the raging creek only to find him dead had long endured. If Kelvin hadn't struck his head on the half-submerged boulders, he could have survived. Life, very sadly, was full of "if onlys."

He had been prepared for the swift onslaught of emotion, but he had to force it aside. He had a job to do. Alex was already well started on her search for her mother's missing jewellery. One could almost give up hope in a house like this, he thought fatalistically. So many rooms, so many hiding places. Everything so disorganized. The library alone was a nightmare. He had grown up in a very different household, where order had reigned.

Kelvin could neither be seen nor heard. There was only a hushed silence. Kelvin had departed the shrine his bereft mother had created in his memory. It seemed that Connor had visited his son's bedroom often, seeking some form of comfort. They had all in their own way kept Kelvin alive, struggling to cope with his death at such a young age and in such a way. He privately thought as he had grown older that the dead needed their deep, sweet sleep as much as anyone else.

Too many memories in this house. Too much unhappiness. The spirit of Kelvin seemed to fill every space. Putting the tragedy of the past aside, he began a systematic search. Kelvin's stock of books came first. He grabbed hold of the collection of comics and put them aside, favouring the books as a possible hiding place. He rifled through *The Lion, the Witch and the Wardrobe*, the first of the Chronicles of Narnia series. Two of the Harry Potter series published before Kelvin died came next. *The Lord of the Rings*. A couple of Dickens. He opened *A Tale of Two Cities*.

"So what's this then?" he said in surprise as a colourful postcard fluttered out of the book and landed on the carpet. It hadn't been stamped nor was there an address written on the right-hand side. The message had been scrawled right across the face of the card. It had to have been sent in an envelope, only there was no envelope, so no clue. He retrieved the card, examining it closely. It read:

Hi Lucy-Lu, What do you know! I've run into a great guy, Italian of course. He's almost as good looking as that guy in all the movies. Mastriano? Vittorio has been showing me all over the island. The beaches are great but not as good as Oz. Seen a few celebs coming out of the very pricey hotels. Fantastic yachts in the marina. Must cost millions. You should be here, girl. You could do well for yourself. No room for anything else. Hugs, Patty.

"Hugs to you too, Patty," Rafe said, turning the postcard to look at the scene again. He had identified it on sight. It was a brilliantly coloured view of the Costa Smeralda, a tourist destination in northern Sardinia. He had visited Italy a number of times over the years, but he had never managed to get to Sardinia, after Sicily the second largest island in the Mediterranean.

So, Lucy-Lu and Patty? Neither name was familiar. What on earth was the postcard doing inside Kelvin's copy of *A Tale of Two Cities*? There was no date, which would have been on the envelope. The handwriting was little more than a scrawl. He knew everyone the Ross children had known. There had never been a Lucy-Lu, let alone a Patty. The card wasn't new or even recent. It was going back some years from the look of it, and curled up at the edges. Had Connor put it there? It was the most likely explanation. Or maybe Rose Anne had? But there again, everyone knew everyone in the town. He continued to sit there, praying hard for enlightenment. There had been no Lucy-Lu on the scene. No Patty. He had found something, so he kept on going.

A stack of birthday cards from Kelvin's little sister, Alex, fell out of *Watership Down*. He sat down on the bed again to read them, taking his time. The cards ran from Kelvin's seventh birthday through to his last, age fourteen. All were written by Alex herself with loving messages, the edges of the cards bordered by little sketches. Brother and sister had been very close, no squabbles, no sibling rivalry, *love*. Time slowed to a crawl . . .

In the end his objective became the close study of Alex's drawings. All of them showed considerable promise, even from age five. Alex was the Rosses' finest achievement. He thought Kelvin would second that. After the longest while he returned the birthday cards to the back of the book. To be honest, he really didn't want to disturb the religious shrine Rose Anne had set up, although there could be something tucked into the back of the numerous framed photographs.

He chose the photos featuring a broadly beaming Connor with his son. None of the snapshots included Alexandra. Frowning in concentration, he separated the photos from the frames. He had no choice but to continue, but it seemed to him the postcard from Sardinia was significant. They could well gain an advantage from his finding it. Connor had spoken to a divorce lawyer. That had come as a shock to all of them. Something had provoked Connor into making such a drastic move. Of course, the postcard might have nothing to do with it.

Kelvin hadn't put the postcard there. Connor must have. He hadn't got rid of it. There had to be *some* connection. He scooped up the comics, put them back in their place. His heart began to pick up speed. He would have *something* to show Alex.

Chapter 6

It wasn't beyond the realm of possibility that there was a false bottom to the antique *cassone* that had always stood at the foot of the marital bed since the house had been built. She and Kelvin had been born a few years after her grandparents had returned to Ireland to take up the estate and a title her grandfather had inherited. She knew primogeniture laws had been changed in recent times, but then and for hundreds of years previously, inheritance had to go through the *male*. Females could be excluded as well by some sort of entail. Women the second-class citizens. Would it ever change?

Word of the rather grand inheritance had come out of the blue. So many men of the O'Farrell line had died in two world wars. From their brief visits to Ireland to meet their grandparents, whom they had adored on sight, Alex knew her grandfather had been a very quirky man, one might say eccentric. Certainly very different to the males of modern society. Her grandparents' lives had been more or less ruled by Old World manners. How to dress, how to speak, how to treat people less fortunate than themselves. The correct setting of the dining room table had been considered important. The exact placement of china and cutlery, wineglasses if they had guests. Even her mother had been a bit of a stickler for the rigid rules of her upbringing. It was her mother who had known this house like no one else did. There could be secret drawers and compartments all over the place. Her mother had once hinted at such without providing details. Maybe she would have told them when they were older. With Kelvin's death that had never happened.

Alex's heart crumpled beneath a swirl of emotions. The heartbreaks and confusion had taken their toll. Very carefully she withdrew everything that was in the chest and placed it on the bed, which still bore its beautiful turquoise silk quilt, though all other bedding had been removed and replaced by new.

Next she turned her attention to prodding at points on the ornately carved chest. She went all around the carved panels, the banded top, the perimeter, and up the sides. Nothing happened. No false bottom then! Another hunch that didn't pay off.

She rose rather shakily to her feet, intending to return the items—the table linens, bed linens, bolts of silk and brocade, a truly exquisite Indian sari—to their resting place. The deep golden embroidery on the silk sari caught her eyes, glittering in the light of the overhead chandelier. It was a gorgeous shade of turquoise with a petticoat that tied at the waist. The shade of the petticoat was obviously meant to deepen the turquoise glow of the silk. A separate cropped top with a deep oval neck and tiny sleeves matched the gold of the sari's deep borders. A sari had to be one of the most elegant forms of attire any woman could wish for, she thought. She wondered if her mother had ever worn it.

She was on the brink of placing the sari on top of the linens she had returned to the chest when she had a strong urge to try it on.

Go on, said the voice in her head. *What do you think is going to happen?*

How perfectly stupid to hold back. She looked down at the exotic garment. The colour was perfect for her. She had never worn such an exquisite garment in all her life. Why not now, while she had the chance? She placed the sari on the bed, twisting her body to drop the heavy top of the antique chest into place. Slightly off balance, knees creaking, she staggered. The tip of her shoe came down hard on one of the chest's paw feet. As she righted herself, with a muffled exclamation, she heard something click.

"Hello, what's that?" Her voice, even to her own ears, sounded wonder struck. Tiny beads of sweat broke out at her temples. She had probed every inch of the chest itself, but not the paw feet. She stared at the chest for a moment, then out came the linens and bolts of fabric. The hidden compartment was now exposed. The honey-coloured timber of the false bottom had sprung open.

It was just as her mother had said. The collection *was* in the antique chest at the foot of her bed. Only Alex realized she would never have found the pad on the claw foot had she been standing firm instead of wobbling on her feet. For long moments she stared as if hypnotised, her eyes ranging over the collection of velvet and wooden boxes that held the family's jewellery collection from generations back.

"You could have told me, Mum," she murmured into the still air. Her expression suggested she was in a dream. Her mother in her own way had been as eccentric as her grandfather. Both had liked magnificent acts of mischief. The valuable family collection had come dangerously close to never being found. At least not by her.

A strange, near defiant, excitement was coming over her as if she had a *right* to be happy. She wasn't going to deny her need. Swiftly she stripped down to her bra and briefs, and then she began the first step to assembling the sari. First she tied the petticoat at her waist. It fell to a level an inch or two above her ankles. Next she slipped into the gold cropped bodice that hooked at the front. It had been made for a very slender woman with a small bust; otherwise it wouldn't have fit. The sari wasn't all that easy to arrange. She had to make several attempts before she got it right, slinging one end over her shoulder as was the tradition. The flat shoes she was wearing didn't look right, so she kicked them off.

The sight of herself in the tall Edwardian pier mirror drew her away from all unhappy thoughts. She pulled out the big comb that had held her hair back, throwing it onto the bed. Her long, thick mane fell free, the blue-black enhancing the palest gold of her skin. She felt incredibly graceful. Incredibly seductive. Completely *woman.*

On an unstoppable roll, she reached for the family treasures, loading herself first off with the family's burning-blue sapphires, necklace and earrings, no bluer than her eyes. The pendant earrings swung from her ears. The necklace, the precious stones set in diamonds, glittered around her throat. Not content with that, she reached for three ropes of pearls, one of which was opera length and fell almost to her waist. She looked quite extraordinary. She felt quite extraordinary. She would go and find Rafe. The fact she had found her mother's jewellery would cheer him up. Certainly her appearance would catch him by surprise. She was all for catching Rafe by surprise. Her whole body felt aglow, tingling right to her fingertips.

Clutching the postcard from Sardinia in his hand, Rafe made his way up the staircase as silent as any cat. He'd visited the Lavender Hill mansion countless times over the long years, but to this very day he couldn't enter the house without thinking, *wow!* As a kid, it had always astonished him Alex and Kelvin hadn't been allowed to wander over to his place as he did to theirs. They had to check if it was okay to arrive unannounced. Then there was the dining routine. Alex and Kelvin wouldn't have dreamt of coming down to breakfast in their pyjamas, even on the weekends. Rose Anne, who had been a very endearing woman, nevertheless had her strict rules. The children had grown up coming down to the breakfast table showered, neatly dressed, and on time. Even Connor had been pulled into line. Poor Connor! He had married way above his station, as one would have said in the old days, although Rose Anne had once surprisingly remarked in his hearing that *all* women married below their station. A closet feminist then, while her daughter was right out in the open.

The huge master bedroom was to his left. It was a room he hadn't entered since the death of Rose Anne. It was a place where any number of secrets could be kept hidden. The hallway was lit up by the sconces, the light falling on pictures and matching pairs of mahogany hall chairs.

He had once suggested to Alex to take the botanical prints down from one wall and replace them with works of her own. She had been horrified. Her mother had had the botanical prints placed there. It was he who had convinced Phillip McHugh, the art dealer, to take a look at Alex's paintings when he came North. The upshot had been that McHugh had offered Alex a showing when she was ready. Alex had a gift. She was wasting it running a mango and lychee plantation. He knew of at least two horticultural experts who could take on the job.

He had almost reached the master bedroom, which in Rose Anne's last months had almost become the epicentre of the house, before he called her name. The door was open, but all was quiet inside. No rustlings, so sound of anything at all. His fingers tightened around the postcard. He hoped with all his heart Alex had found her mother's jewellery. The collection had great sentimental value.

"Alex?" His voice sounded unnaturally loud. It resounded down the long, empty corridor with its rather unsettling atmosphere of shadows. At least he would have something to show for his time. He tried to make light of it, but he had the most extraordinary sense of being caught up in some mystical experience. His mother had once said Lavender Hill had a magic ring around it. That was before Kelvin...

He moved to the bedroom doorway, his breath catching in his throat. Alex stood only a few feet inside. To his dazzled eyes she stood covered in the most marvellous jewels of all colours. He saw sapphires and diamonds, rubies and pearls, some golden stones he thought might be topaz, all glittering and shimmering at the ears, throat, and breast of a most beautiful woman. The protectiveness he had always felt for Alex since childhood alchemized in seconds into a white-hot desire.

She was wearing an exquisite turquoise blue sari, the gold border iridescent where it caught the light. Where had she got it? It was wonderfully becoming to her. A gold-coloured bodice beneath closely moulded her perfect breasts. The colours were picked up and enhanced by the furnishings of the opulent Old World bedroom with its walls covered in gold damask. The floor-to-ceiling drapes and the quilt on the ornate Victorian bed were a deeper shade of turquoise silk. The glitter of the cut-glass swags and drops of the Waterford chandelier fell directly on her and were reflected in the gilt mirrors. But it was the woman who commanded attention.

That was the great genius of this fantasy house—this fantasy woman. He was fanatically in love with Alex. He had been since forever. Maybe from the beginning of time. Alex was his and his alone. He took a deep breath, letting it out very slowly. "You *are* here, aren't you?" he asked, not without humour.

She didn't speak. It was as if she didn't know what to say.

He knew he couldn't stop what was about to happen. His energy was like a molten stream coursing through his veins. He could see she was trembling. He himself felt tremors rocking his body. He moved towards her. She didn't retreat.

"You only have to tell me to stop, Alex," he said. That, when he was certain he had forgotten how to.

Again she didn't answer, but her slender body appeared full of a desperate yearning.

Slowly he moved in, wondering if she would reconsider and begin to struggle against him. Only everything began to slot into place. The ultimate moment had arrived. With a soft growl he pulled her into his arms, making no attempt to mask the fierceness of his emotions.

"Stop me, Alex," he softly challenged, staring down into her beautiful blue eyes. He had no intention of ever being pushed away again.

The one passionate kiss they had shared had prepared her for what was to follow. He wanted her. He wanted every part of her. The magnificent sapphire and diamond necklace glittered on her breast. He let his hand trail down to touch it. He was fascinated by all the jewellery she had piled on. Impossible to ascertain the value. Thousands and thousands. A rope of lustrous pearls swung to her waist. More fat, lustrous pearls adorned her flawless skin.

With ease, he picked up her unresisting body and carried her across the room to the bed. At the last moment he slung her over his shoulder so her long hair stroked his back. Swiftly he yanked off the silk quilt. The bed's furnishings, all new, had the fresh smell of the native boronia.

He laid her down, watching her roll modestly on her side. She had made no gesture to indicate his actions were unwelcome, although she had to know where all this was leading. This was the marriage bed of her family. He sat down on the side of the bed, turning her so he could meet her eyes. She gazed back at him in the profound silence, as though she needed a moment to catch her breath.

When he could hold off no longer, he bent his head over her, breathing in her fragrance for a moment, before he captured her beautiful, cushiony mouth. The level of hunger in him was dangerously high. He longed to possess her but he knew it had to be in the manner Alex craved. He could take her in heat or he could take her slowly. Her whole body twisted and her legs moved restlessly as his hands moved down over her breasts.

No matter how exquisite the sari, it had to come off. She recognized that, helping him as he turned her this way and that. He was far more adept at it than he would have thought. Finally the petticoat and bodice remained. Her cheeks were blushed. Her blue eyes glittered as blue as the precious stones. Emotion made them appear exceptionally large.

"This rope will have to come off," he said, fingering the waist-length strand of pearls. "I don't want the string to break, scattering pearls all over the place."

She breathed a soft cry as he lifted her head to remove the lustrous rope, twisting to lay it on the bedside table, one of two that formed the bedroom suite. All the rest of the jewellery could stay in place. He was finding it unbearably, unutterably exciting that she keep it on. She tried to help him as he unhooked the gold bodice and then her bra. He had no difficulty with the petticoat and briefs. He had seen her naked years ago when she was skinny-dipping in the creek, her long black hair trailing like a pennant, thinking herself alone. Now she was a woman. All woman.

She half rose, with muffled little cries that incited him to the breaking point. She was caressing his head with her hand. Her hand still holding him, she pressed his face and his lips to her naked breasts, moaning as he took her tender nipples into his mouth, one after the other.

It was all he could do to hold back. She was bringing him too perilously close to man's primitive mastery over woman. He pulled away, standing up so he could swiftly slough off his own clothes. The powerful muscles of his back and shoulders were bunched, his long legs and his thighs quivering with the sheer effort of controlling his frantic sexual drive. He climbed back onto the bed, crouching over her, holding his lean, taut body away from hers with the strength of his arms. Then he allowed his body to come down on hers.

Immediately she wrapped her slender arms around him while her long, beautiful legs came up around his thighs to clutch his body to hers. He was very close to entering her, waiting for the exact moment when her need of him was unmistakable. Her whole body was bucking beneath his ministrations. He was deliberately driving her to the point where she couldn't contain herself.

"Please, Rafe, *please*." Her plea came to him, infinitely soft, infinitely desirous. Her long fingers reached down to enclose his rock hard shaft, guiding him into her. It was enough to bring his urgency to a crescendo. The lips of her pulsing vagina were tight as he began his thrust, and their bodies became one. For a moment he was afraid he might hurt her, but gradually they were moving in unison, half delirious with their lovemaking, both on the verge of a shattering orgasm.

He heard himself cry out, a shattered yet triumphant, "Aaaah!" as he exploded deep inside her.

It was the time. It was total. It was infinite ecstasy.

He awoke in the pre-dawn from long habit. For a split second he felt disoriented. Where was his slate-grey and white, very masculine bedroom? His eyes always fell first on a huge framed photograph of a famous Australian racehorse on the wall directly facing him. Now it fell on a fantastic four-leaf Coromandel screen, gilded black lacquer painted with flowering trees, tiny bluebirds in the branches, tall standing white cranes. His sense of place rocketed back in, as did the powerful storm of memories of all that had happened during the night.

Alex lay fast asleep beside him, her long black eyelashes fanning her beautiful skin. Alex! There was no place on earth he would rather be than beside her. He gazed down at her, spellbound, desperately moved, scarcely able to believe their perfect night together. Her body was turned towards his. Her outstretched hand slid off his shoulder as he very slowly began to move. They had made love all through the night, drowsing off for short, satiated periods, seeking each other out, time and time again.

He allowed the strong impulse to pull her into his arms to ebb. She needed valuable sleep. God knows how many matters he had had to put aside, which now needed his attention. He hoped Amy, in hospital, would wake feeling better. Her mother was due to arrive around midday. He and Alex would meet her at the airport and bring her back to the hospital to see her daughter. No doubt the mother would be extremely upset. Even more so if and when she found out the intended victim had been Alex. If Bob Ralston was responsible, he would be easily caught and charged.

The way he saw it, Sasha wouldn't do anything to jeopardize her chances of winning a large settlement. The big worry now was if her very astute lawyer might be able to make a good case for her. There was a weight of evidence recently that seemingly air-tight wills were contested in the courts. Some cases, involving big money, had dragged on for years. Connor's widow was potentially dangerous. He hadn't told Alex about the postcard he had found. Last night the postcard was the last thing on his mind. He would show it to her on their way to the airport. He wondered if Alex would have any idea who "Lucy-Lu" and "Patty" were.

Chapter 7

Alex snapped awake and sat up, naked save for a wealth of her mother's jewellery draped around her neck and swinging from her ears. She called Rafe's name on a soft, urgent note. He wasn't in the bed beside her. There was no answer—only a deep quiet. Taking stock of the situation, she began to remove the pendant earrings and the multiple necklaces, placing them carefully on the bed. A ray of sun hit them with full-spectrum glitter so their glory was almost decadent. So was her nakedness. Her face and her entire body flushed as she thought of all that had taken place the night before. She actually had found proof that her world could be this side of paradise.

Turning her head to the nightstand, she saw it was already eight fifteen. A note was weighed down by a Baccarat pansy paper weight. She rolled sideways to reach it.

Gone home to attend to a few things. Will pick you up 10:45 sharp. R.

So back to business then! No mention of their rhapsodically life-changing night. It was all a dream, yet her body told her very differently. She still felt electrically charged. She could still feel him inside her. Her breasts still felt the weight of his hands.

Only there was no time to dwell on what enthralling things had happened. She had to shower, shampoo her wildly tousled hair, and get dressed to meet Mrs. Bateman, Amy's mother, at the airport, a good hour's drive away.

She moved swiftly after that, returning the jewellery collection to its various boxes, then placing them in the secret compartment, pressing down the lid.

She was out of the bathroom, pulling out suitable clothes, black-and-white striped cotton capris with a white pleated cotton blouse, when she heard movement downstairs. That would be Mrs. Pidgeon, her recent ally. She needed a couple of cups of blistering hot, blistering strong coffee to keep her focused.

When Rafe arrived, she was waiting for him on the veranda. He moved out of the Range Rover, starting towards her with his long, elegant strides. She met him halfway. He didn't swoop down to kiss her, even on her cheek. He said briskly, "Come on, we've got things to talk about."

"Right you are, Captain." She slipped into the passenger seat. "I'm glad to see the old Rafe returning," she half joked as they moved off.

"The new Rafe only comes out at night." He swept her a brilliant, all-encompassing glance. "Here, take a look at this." He handed over a postcard.

"One of your lady friends? I know for a fact there's at least a score or more of hopefuls."

He gave her a half smile. "I'm sorry if I'm popular with the ladies. Actually I don't know who it is," he said with a slight frown. "I thought you might."

"Will we still be friends after I read it?" She glanced at the shot of beautiful Sardinia.

"We're not *friends*, Alex. I thought it had been established. We're soul mates."

"That's all right then." It was as if his arms had closed around her. She turned the postcard over, commenting on the scrawl. "Lucy-Lu? Patty? Has your past caught up with you?"

"If it has, I don't recognize the names. I found it last night in Kel's room. It fell out of a book. *Lord of the Rings*, to be precise."

"So who put it there?" she asked in surprise. "I don't know any Lucy-Lu or a Patty. How did it come to be there? It has nothing to do with Kelvin."

"I suspect your father shoved it in there," Rafe said. "I have no idea why. You look beautiful, by the way."

The note in his voice put a tremble in her fingers. "Thank you. I should warn you, Mrs. Bateman is quite a *personage*. She was very upset when I spoke to her. She didn't exactly blame me for not looking after Amy properly, but a hint of an accusation was there. The police will have spoken to Amy this morning. Do you suppose they've made the connection to me?"

"Of course they have. They couldn't disregard the possibility that Bob Ralston might have been trying to frighten you."

"Do you think they'll pass their suspicions on to Amy?" she asked, not altogether confident they wouldn't.

"I've asked them to be discreet."

"It *will* come out."

"Bound to," he agreed with a shrug. "Hopefully by which time the police will have Ralston in custody. But to get back to Lucy-Lu? I'm convinced that postcard means something."

"A secret about a secret," Alex said.

"Why else had it been concealed in a book in Kelvin's room? Your father visited the room often. Could the postcard have been sent to Sasha?"

"It's not dated, unfortunately. No envelope to give us a clue?"

"No."

"What a pity. Most people send postcards stamped and addressed. But not this time. It's not new. It looks some years old."

"How do we know Sasha and Lucy-Lu aren't one and the same?" Rafe offered.

Alex exhaled a long breath. "That's a bit of a leap."

"Wrong answer. I go on my instincts. Sasha could have been careless leaving it around. Connor might have come across the postcard, read it, and then asked Sasha who these people were—her friends? Remember, she appears very short of them."

"Okay." Alex took a moment to consider. "She could have simply said Lucy-Lu was a friend of hers from way back. So was Patty. Lucy had showed her the postcard and she had inadvertently held on to it for years."

He gave her a taut smile. "How come your dad didn't believe her?"

Alex didn't have to think hard. "I suppose because she's a bit of a liar."

"Bit of!" he scoffed.

"You should have been a detective, Rafe."

"Might I remind you, you need one," he retorted. "You already have one on the job. Healey is a big-time lawyer. We can rely on Sasha, who may or may not have the alias Lucy-Lu, to play dirty.

She's out for all she can get, an epic settlement just like the ones she reads about. I'm going to send this piece of information on to our investigator."

"How many Lucys do you suppose were born in New Zealand—in what?" Alex queried. "Sasha claims she's thirty-seven."

"And the rest. Say she's in her early forties, which brings us back to the early nineteen seventies. That should narrow it down."

"Even if Sasha turns out to be Lucy, what does that tell us?"

"My most beautiful, gorgeous, darling Alexandra," he taunted, "Sasha believed it was in her karma to marry a rich man."

Alex was so high up she thought she would never come down. *Beautiful. Gorgeous. Darling.* "Sasha didn't give a toss it took her into her forties to achieve her goal?" she said, when she settled. "I have to question that. She couldn't have been in a convent in the years in between. She's a very pretty woman."

"A sexpot on the loose," Rafe commented, very dryly.

"You should never have encouraged her, sweet prince."

He gave her a twisted white smile. "You know what they say about sarcasm, Ms. Ross. I'd say Sasha has been involved with quite a few men over the past twenty-plus years."

"Very likely, but how does that help us unless she ran over one. Like she tried to run *me* off the road."

"So she organised a hire car then took it back with the off side bashed in? Sasha isn't behind the cowardly attack, Alex. I know it. She thinks she's on to a good thing." He glanced at her. "You want to tell me why your father made an appointment with a divorce lawyer?"

"If there was ever anyone to find out, it would be you."

"Through our good friend Max. He won't even have to lean hard on your father's divorce lawyer."

"Maybe Dad didn't give a reason. He just wanted a divorce. Doesn't it come down to irreconcilable differences? No fault?"

"They continued to live under the one roof. They may have continued to share the same bed for all we know. Though that doesn't sound like your father once he had considered divorce. He certainly didn't tell Sasha he wanted a divorce. He was being very secretive. What for? What did he have on Sasha? For that matter, what was—for want of a better word—her maiden name?"

"Stevens. Sasha Stevens. Nice ring to it. Dad didn't tell anyone what was on his mind. Nothing new about that. But did he actually intend to proceed? We'll never know."

"Something brought about the change in him, Alex," Rafe mused. "Something hit him hard enough to seek out a good divorce lawyer. He even went as far afield as Sydney."

"He didn't love her, Rafe. Not the day he married her. Not the day he died. The only person my father ever truly loved was Kelvin."

"Well, *me*"—he turned his handsome face toward her—"I love his daughter. I've always loved her. And finally, last night, I got her to admit she loves *me*."

She felt the quick blush from her head to her toes. "When did I do that?"

His laugh came from low in his chest. "I admit it's taken a while, but last night your need was too great. Have you forgotten the whimpers, the little moans into my mouth? You didn't say, *I love you*?"

"I must have," she said shakily. "It's all a *huge* swirl in my head."

He reached for her hand, linking her fingers through his. "Swirl or not, you can never take it back."

"You'll have your hands full with me, Rafe Rutherford," she warned, looking down at their linked hands.

"Don't I know it! I also know I'm up to the challenge."

Her breath came deeper. "So we're a pair?"

Rafe glanced at her sidelong, his heart in his eyes. "Alex, we always were."

Mrs. Bateman, a dead ringer for the late Iron Lady, Margaret Thatcher, was one of those women who exuded all the self-assurance of a long-standing member of the so-called Establishment. She was not a woman in touch with the common people. Alex entertained the thought that Sasha would wither beneath one of Mrs. Bateman's piercing blue stares.

Alex had got to know Mrs. Bateman quite well during her university days, but that lady, while always gracious and welcoming, had never unbent. Protocol had to be upheld. There had been no question of ever addressing Mrs. Bateman as Barbara, though Amy's father had told her smilingly, the first time they met, to please call him Peter.

Mrs. Bateman stepped off the domestic flight as fresh and uncreased as the moment she boarded. She was wearing a designer-label white linen suit with a smart navy-and-white patterned silk blouse beneath. Her fashionable ash-blond hair—Barbara Bateman was a natural blue-eyed blonde—was worn in a chin-length, thick pageboy. Amy had not taken after her mother in looks or manner. Amy was more her father's side of the family with her dark hair, dark eyes, and egalitarian manner.

It was quiet in the car on the drive to the hospital, the atmosphere edgy with not quite hostility emanating from the back seat. Alex had not been greeted with a *lovely to see you, dear*. Rafe had been paid rather more attention, though Mrs. Bateman had not favoured either of them with smiles. For the most part she had remained grim faced, clearly exceedingly worried about her only daughter. On arrival at the airport, Rafe had given her the latest report to ease her concerns. No matter! Mrs. Bateman, like doubting Thomas, had to see with her own eyes.

Thankfully Amy had had a good night. She was free to leave hospital that morning. Barbara Bateman had made it clear that she wanted to see her daughter first before any decisions were made.

"A hit-and-run!" She had cast her eyes to Heaven. "I can't believe it. What sort of person would do that? All I want is to see my daughter."

Mrs. Bateman sat in the back of the car, staring out at the verdant green miles without making any comment about the beauty and uniqueness of the tropical landscape or the extraordinary illumination of the tropical sun. Alex felt it was all Mrs. Bateman could do not to come out into the open and blame someone, maybe *partially* blame her, for Amy's accident. Barbara Bateman had come North for one reason only. To take her daughter back to the safety of their home in Brisbane. There had been no mention whatever of Alex being the intended victim, so that piece of information the police had kept to themselves. One had to be grateful for small mercies.

Amy was already dressed in the blue lightweight tracksuit Alex had couriered to the hospital to make dressing easier for her friend. She was sitting in a wheelchair out in the corridor when they arrived. Mrs. Bateman all but ran down the aisle, Alex and Rafe following slowly. Alex could actually see Amy gulp at her mother's approach.

Alex had learned, although it had never been put into words, that Amy found her mother's possessiveness difficult to deal with.

The doctor who had attended Amy when she was brought in was called for and collared for a discussion. "I told you not to ring Mother, Alex," Amy whispered behind her hand. "She makes such a big deal of everything."

"She loves you, Amy. She's been terribly worried." Alex patted her friend's shoulder.

"That would be good if she didn't make such a fuss," said an embarrassed Amy, who appeared freaked out by her own mother. "The doctor and staff have been very good to me here, yet just look at Mother. You'd think she was going to have the doctor up on a charge."

Alex had to admit it did look a bit like a soldier standing at attention while his superior officer demanded explanations.

"Bit of a Tartar, our Mrs. Bateman." Rafe leaned closer to Alex, a wry smile playing around his chiselled mouth. Amy continued to stare off rather frantically in the direction of the doctor and her hectoring mother. "Doc Martin by now would have told her to lay off," said Rafe. "I'd happily put her in her place myself, only she's Amy's mother."

"We have to remember that. Perhaps she will settle down when she realizes Amy will recover quickly, though God knows the outcome could have been very different," Alex said with a shudder.

It was only when they arrived back at the estate that Mrs. Bateman finally unwound sufficiently to comment on the beauty of the tropical landscape. Her first view of the house put her into relative raptures.

"Of course I've seen the photographs in Historic Homesteads," she informed them, "but they don't do the house justice. Why, it's as romantic a colonial mansion as one could wish for."

Thank God for that, thought Alex.

The graceful jacarandas that surrounded the house had begun breaking out into their intense lavender-blue blossom. The sight stirred Amy's mother into further praise. She even lowered her window, unmindful of the hot rush of air and the certainty of wind-blown hair.

Rafe saw them into the house before excusing himself with practised charm, but the glance he shot in Alex's direction said plainly, *I'm outta here!*

"What an extraordinarily attractive young man," Barbara Bateman said, now widely smiling. "A close friend of yours, Alex?" She spoke archly, as though she were a mind reader.

"I've known Rafe all my life," Alex said. "We grew up together, though he's four years older."

"I wouldn't let him get away, dear." Mrs. Bateman looked into Alex's eyes as though imparting great wisdom.

Amy gave her friend a light clap on the back. "Atta girl!"

Alex couldn't stop herself from laughing, but she managed to quickly sober. "Let me show you to your room, Mrs. Bateman. I've put you beside Amy. I hope you'll be very comfortable. If you need anything you have only to ask."

"Lovely!" Mrs. Bateman had completely thawed out; in fact, she was far more gushing than Alex had ever seen her. "I can't wait to see the house. It's quite Somerset Maugham-ish, isn't it? That fishbowl on its stand is simply gorgeous. Kangxi period, I expect."

She was spot-on. Alex glanced at her clever, confident friend, who was lagging behind her mother like a little girl. "Would you like to lie down for a while, lovey?" she said tenderly. "I can have something sent up to you. Tea, coffee?"

"No, I'll come down."

"If you're sure. I'll have Mrs. Pidgeon make morning tea. Say, fifteen minutes."

Amy winked at her. "Say *ten*."

Mrs. Bateman proved to be a dedicated houseguest. "Peter, of course, is a fiercely busy man, but he would love to look over the estate."

Alex responded that he would be more than welcome. Mrs. Bateman was also showing an unprecedented interest in Alex's life. It was obvious Amy had told her mother nothing about Connor Ross's missing will or the strong possibility he had died intestate. Alex was grateful for that. To add to their guest's enjoyment, Mrs. Pidgeon kept up the supply of fresh salmon and perfectly scrambled farm eggs, arguably Mrs. Bateman's favourite dish.

Mrs. Bateman did know Alex had lost her brother, Kelvin, when they were children, so she had the delicate sensibility not to attempt to venture into Kelvin's room. It was the only room she found sacrosanct. She was by now liberated from her fears that her beloved daughter had suffered grievous bodily harm, so that by the time to leave the following day for the flight back to Brisbane, Mrs. Bateman was able to give Alex a swift kiss. Rafe, who had driven them to the airport, also received a kiss on the cheek and an affectionate hug.

Amy, looking a little drained and pale, appeared dispirited to be leaving. "I mean, you're going to let me know what's happening?" she asked Alex, who was holding her friend's hand to stop her twisting her hands in her lap.

"Of course I am, love. I'm going to ring every day to check on how you're feeling. It grieves me terribly you had such an awful experience. I'll e-mail you as well," Alex promised. "If I have big news, I'll ring you at the office."

"Sorry about Mother," Amy apologized yet again. "I love her. She's my mother. One always loves one's mother. I hate to say it, but I don't like her. Isn't that awful? She's such a snob. I thought she was never going to shut up about all the antiques."

"Your mother knows her stuff," Alex, who had thought the same, said in a conciliatory tone.

"And hasn't she taken to Rafe?"

"Every woman does." Alex spoke very dryly.

"You love him." Amy put intense emphasis on the *love*.

"Of course I do. I owe him a staggering debt."

Amy kept her golden-brown eyes on her friend. "I think you should consider how much you're *in love* with him, Lexie," she said. "Because it's the truth, isn't it?"

Alex didn't say anything for a moment. She really wanted to hug her epiphany to herself. At least for a time until she got halfway used to what had happened to her.

"Okay, so?" Amy prompted.

"When I can see the light at the end of the tunnel, I promise you, Amy, you'll be the first to know."

"I'm pretty darn sure I know already," said Amy, whose own hopes and dreams had blown away on the wind.

She was alone at the Lodge for the day. Rafe had gone off to attend to one of his many deferred business matters. "You'll go home then?" she had asked, waiting on his answer. The last thing she wanted to appear was clingy. She'd always prided herself on her independence; she still did.

His white smile glittered. He looked down at her with half-closed eyes. "No chance of that, Alex."

She felt the colour rush to her cheeks. "Okay then."

He hadn't kissed her. He'd trailed a finger down her cheek. The kisses would come later. Theirs was no halfhearted relationship many couples got by on. They had been through too many crises. She saw as he did. He saw as she did. That was the kind of man she had always needed.

She had turned one large room in the Lodge into her studio. There was as much light as possible in the room. It came from a large window to one side and French doors on the other, covering both north and south across the plantation, both offering spectacular views. She stood for long moments with her arms folded across her breasts. An unfinished watercolour stood on an easel. It depicted a jabiru, Australia's black-necked stork with striking black-and-white plumage, deep red legs, and its feet were standing in a glassy green pool with open rainforest as a background. She really would have to finish it. It was good. She did have confidence in her work, her ability to draw and paint.

She loved her watercolours, a difficult medium, only she knew who she wanted to paint that afternoon in the traditional oils. She felt bold. She knew her subject intimately, but how to best capture him on canvas? Rafe's head and wide shoulders filled her mind. He was a very handsome man, but handsome didn't say it. It was what was *inside* the man she wanted to paint. She could see his brilliant dark eyes, the arch of his brows, the chiselled features, his shapely mouth, his thick, crow-black hair that had a natural deep wave, his fine olive skin. She could see the set of his shoulders. She could actually sense him so strongly he might have been standing beside her. Rafe Rutherford, her closest, dearest friend, her lover, the hero of her childhood. If she wanted romance with real passion, she had experienced it right to the depths of her soul.

The stretched canvas was resting on a larger easel. She would be using oils. Her palette with her brushes lay on the table. There was a technique to painting in whatever medium. She had studied them all in many nighttime art classes. She was confident of her sketching ability, getting the main elements of her model's face onto the canvas. Then she could go to work bringing her subject to life. It was rare she felt unsure of herself before starting a new work, but this was Rafe. She wanted to capture his very *essence*. She wanted to do it so well he would be ready to step out of the canvas. The key elements of Rafe's face were his brilliant, near-black eyes and arched black eyebrows. His hair was important. She planned on painting it longer, with more curl than he normally allowed. She had to get the flesh colour right, his polished olive skin deepened to tan by a tropical sun. She wanted to reproduce her romantic hero. Painting Rafe would be a little like making love to him. She had the artist's intimation this would be her best work.

Late that afternoon, Rafe called in at the police station to see if there was any news. Constable Mary McGregor, pleasant and efficient, was at the desk gossiping with a male colleague, who moved off fast. She informed him with a smile that Sergeant Atkinson would be pleased to see him. She led the way.

Atkinson, in his late fifties, heaved his burly frame out of his swivel chair to shake hands as the constable closed the door. Cliff Atkinson was a kindly man, but Rafe knew he could be very tough when he had to be. "Sit down, Rafe," he invited, rubbing his eyes. The sergeant was looking like he had had no sleep at all. "We've checked out Ralston, needless to say. Any number of witnesses in the pub where he was drinking Wednesday afternoon. He walked into town and walked out. Again witnesses. We've checked his Toyota. It's just as he claimed, broken down, in need of repairs. He hadn't had anything done because he was broke and he owed money to the garage. We checked. He does. He had heard about Ms. Bateman's accident, of course. He sounded genuinely shocked."

"Did he now!" Rafe said. "I'd say he was genuinely shocked it wasn't Alex."

Atkinson shrugged. "He wasn't driving that afternoon, Rafe. Apart from anything else, he wasn't in any fit state to. We checked Frank de Campo out as well. We've caught Frank driving over the limit, but he had an alibi, which we verified. He'd heard about the accident, of course. Everyone has. The thing is, no one in town would harm Alex, Rafe. The whole thing is as unbelievable as it was deliberate."

"And Mrs. Ross?"

Atkinson hesitated. "Not a mark on her very expensive Merc, as one would suspect. All her comings and goings have been marked. She wasn't at all helpful. In fact she started jumping up and down about police harassment and what she would do about it. She's a piece of work, that one. I suppose I can understand why Connor fell into the trap, but it surely couldn't have taken him long to regret it."

"Charlie Wilson has an old ute," Rafe suddenly thought, not about to pick up on Cliff's comment.

Atkinson sat up straighter, looking like a man who might have missed something. "Charlie? Charlie is away on a fishing trip."

"I know. All the same, I'd run a check on his ute. I do recall seeing Ralston driving it a good while back. That's when they were reasonably friendly. It's not impossible Ralston may have borrowed it. He has really gone downhill."

"No three ways to Sunday, he's messed up," Atkinson agreed. "He has never threatened Alex?"

"No, Cliff, but there's little doubt he blames her for losing his job."

"He was certainly well over the limit when he left the pub. No secret to that. Could he have driven any vehicle at all?"

"He'd be fool enough to try if he caught sight of Alex's Mercedes somewhere on the road."

"Ralston is just so damn nasty, so belligerent, it's hard to feel sorry for him. Zack Owens sacked him as well. Should Zack be on the lookout?"

"It's *women* Ralston targets." Rafe showed his contempt.

Atkinson shook his head. "His missus never did charge him with abuse, no matter how bad things got."

"Why she didn't remains a mystery," said Rafe. "But she did finally get away. Let's hope to something better."

"Amen to that. I'll take a run out to Charlie's place," Atkinson said. "The ute is always in the carport."

Rafe nodded. "It's worth a shot. Ralston could have been just mad enough to think he could get away with scaring Alex if he used Charlie's ute as cover."

"You want a coffee?" Atkinson asked.

"If you're having one."

"Anything with it?"

"No, thanks." Rafe liked Cliff Atkinson and his team. "You

know, Cliff, you look tired. I'm passing Charlie's place. Let me take a look. If I find anything I'll ring you."

"Let's look together," said Atkinson.

Edna Mitchell stared anxiously out her back window. At this time of year it was a sea of gold. Charlie Wilson's mother, Alice, had once had the idea of starting a sunflower farm, but her husband and son weren't interested in that. Uninterested or not, the sunflowers Alice had planted had taken off, as sunflowers do. Over the years the flowers had spread over a huge area, delighting the eye. No wonder that Dutch fellow had been obsessed with painting his sunflowers, Edna thought. They were glorious.

She could see Bob Ralston ducking and weaving across the golden field like a man who was trying hard not to be seen. It suddenly occurred to her where he was going. Over to Charlie's place, of course. Charlie was away on a fishing trip. Everyone in town knew that. She didn't know if Ralston had clearance from the police or not. That poor girl could have been killed and it could have been Alexandra. In a town like theirs, everyone knew everyone else's business, so everyone knew Ralston blamed Alexandra for giving him the sack. Ralston was not a man of good character. She knew for a fact he had often given his wife a backhander, though she had never reported him to the police. No wonder the poor woman had run off with some itinerant worker.

Edna stepped purposefully away from her window, thinking she would get something out in the open. She went directly to the phone in the hallway and put a call through to the police station. If Ralston was innocent he had nothing to worry about. The hit-and-run driver had obviously thought it was Alexandra at the wheel. Edna didn't think she would ever get over the shock of seeing that other girl, at first thinking it was Alexandra, who she had known from babyhood. Edna knew in her bones Ralston would delight in giving Alexandra a good scare. He was that kind of man. His ute was out of action. That meant he had to find another vehicle. Why not Charlie Wilson's old bomb? At least it ran, for all the state it was in.

Cliff Atkinson took the call in his car. She was a shrewd old girl, Edna Mitchell, though she had to be well into her eighties. So Ralston was on his way to Charlie Wilson's farm? He could see Rafe's

Range Rover in his rear-vision mirror. He would indicate they would pull over at the entrance to the farm and do their own traipsing up to the house. This trip was by no means a waste of time.

They say a criminal almost always returns to the scene of the crime. Charlie's farm wasn't the scene of the crime, but it was where the vehicle involved stood in the carport gathering more dust. He had to check on it. It was a compulsion he couldn't conquer. These past days he had become unbelievably anxious he was going to be caught. His alibi for that afternoon had stood up. He had witnesses. No one had seen him driving Charlie's old ute. No sightings whatever, or someone would have come forward.

He knew the lord of the valley, Rafe Rutherford, had been hell-bent on tracking his movements, so it must have been a huge disappointment to him to find Bob Ralston was in the clear. The thing was, some of his bloody neighbours had their eye on him as well. Old Edna Mitchell, for one. She who had first come on the accident and reported it, like the busybody she was. The old girl had to be nearly ninety. The rear of her cottage faced onto the sunflower field. The flowers were prodigious—big, bright yellow-gold, standing in some places over his head—but old Edna was probably as blind as a bat even with her specs on. But he knew he should have worn his baseball cap pulled down hard over his eyes. It was too late now.

He would make a fast check on the damage. It was helpful Charlie's ute was even more battered than his. It was all too easy to hit a kangaroo or a wallaby if the silly buggers took it into their heads to hop out on the road, only to stand transfixed before an oncoming vehicle. Of course there were signs letting motorists know the spots kangaroos liked to cross, but he mostly ignored them. Save the kangaroos. Save the koalas. Save the whales. To hell with the lot of them! It was all a waste of time.

Rafe and the sergeant drove up to the edge of the Wilson farm. The long line of timber fencing that fronted onto the country road was only just kept upright by a dense outer wall of magenta bougainvillea that spilled down onto the thick grass of the verge.

Stealthily they made their way up to the house. They needed to catch Ralston in the act of inspecting Wilson's ute. What was left of Alice Wilson's once thriving garden provided good cover: all her shrubs and bushes, the spectacular carissas, the hibiscus, the ficus, the oleanders and the frangipani, all in flower and heavy with scent. They could see Ralston moving up and down the left side of Charlie Wilson's ute. He was going over it inch by inch. Atkinson signalled to Rafe. Time to confront their suspected hit-and-run driver.

Apprehension couldn't have been easier.

"Well, well, well, Bob, fancy finding you here," Sergeant Atkinson called in a friendly fashion.

Ralston reacted with horror. "Just checking on me mate Charlie's ute," he explained, lifting a dirty hand to brush away the sweat that was blinding his eyes.

"Find everything okay?" Rafe asked, as the two six-foot-plus men closed in on Ralston.

"Come here. Take a look at this," Ralston invited. "That's one cold-blooded bastard who ran that poor girl off the road."

"One cold-blooded bastard like you, Bob," Atkinson said, reaching his man and patting him hard on the shoulder. "You might have killed her."

"Me?" Ralston blurted, about to go into full panic mode. "I wouldn't kill anyone."

"Well, maybe not kill, but run off the road. A witness has come forward, Bob my man. One of you is lying. I know it's not the witness. You're cooked like a chook. Let's take a look, shall we, at what damage you inflicted on Wilson's ute. He'll be none too pleased about that."

Ralston broke into his store of choice language. "The bloody ute couldn't be in worse condition," he finished with a total lack of shame.

"Don't worry, Bob, we'll find enough traces of silver paint." Atkinson made the confident promise.

"Was it that old bitch Edna Mitchell who saw me?" Ralston snarled.

Police Sergeant Atkinson shook his head. "It wasn't, Bob. Unusual conclusion for an old lady who wears specs."

Ralston started to unravel. "I never saw no one. Not a glimpse," he glared, his face red from drink and the heat. "I didn't want to hurt her, I swear. I just wanted to scare her. She did me out of a job."

"You thought it was Ms. Ross then, in the car?" Sergeant Atkinson asked.

"Don't blame me for making a mistake. From a distance that other bloody girl could have been her. Miss High and Mighty sacked me. Kicked a man when he was down."

"Zack Owens sacked you as well," Rafe pointed out. "Were you going to get square with him as well?"

"It's women. Bloody women who give the most aggro," Ralston fiercely maintained. "You can bust me, but I still say Miss High and Mighty had it comin'."

Rafe couldn't help it. Without moving, he gave Ralston a good clip over the ear. "Tell that to the judge, Ralston."

Ralston looked back at the police sergeant with genuine horror. "You saw that, Sergeant Atkinson. He *hit* me."

Atkinson, well pleased with the afternoon's events, raised surprised brows. "I saw nothing. You should knock off the booze, Bob. Now, of course, you'll have to. We're going to take a little walk back to the police car. I'm not going to cuff you unless I have to. It's in your own interests not to cause any further trouble. Got that?"

Ralston snorted, but he went quietly. Life had gone so grievously wrong he didn't care if he did wind up in jail. He had a couple of mates inside; though, on second thought, he doubted they would welcome him. Charlie would spot the fresh damage anyway and settle on him for the culprit. He could even hear his ex-mate Charlie say *Good riddance to bad rubbish!*

Chapter 8

Alex was so completely engrossed in her work she didn't hear Rafe park the Range Rover outside the Lodge. She had been painting for hours, watching the portrait take shape and come to life. Never had she been so inspired. She had done numerous sketches of Rafe's handsome head over the years. At the bottom of it, even during childhood, was her fascination for him. The light from the large window fell directly on the painting on the easel. It was Amy who had put the notion into her head: Rafe bore a strong resemblance to the Irish actor who played Ross Poldark in the TV series. The Rutherford ancestors were Scottish. Arguably the best James Bond had been the Scot Sean Connery—whose colouring as a young man was the same as Rafe's, right down to the brilliant dark eyes.

She had further conceived the idea of showing a glimpse of the tropical landscape through the large open window, a point of interest beyond the dominating central character. Arms folded, she had stared at the painting for some time. It was astonishing how realistic it was.

She stepped back a foot or so to view the painting as a whole. She had intended to dress Rafe in a casual, open-necked white shirt. She *loved* white. White could be used to enormous advantage. In the end she had switched to the full-sleeved white shirt of a bygone age. She had lengthened his black waving hair as well, tying it back in a ponytail. It increased the illusion of another time. A very striking, romantic-looking man met her eyes.

The painting of his head and torso wasn't complete, of course. It needed more work; even so, it could have stood alone. It made her happy the painting revealed a lot of professionalism as well as innate artistry. When it was finished, she would sign it in the lower right-hand corner.

That she had been able to tell Rafe, even if it had been in an agonized, heart-wrenching way, that she loved him, had gone the whole way to cauterizing her wounds. Once she had lamented that she loved Rafe, taking it as a burden she had to carry. Now she acknowledged with absolute certainty she loved him and wanted to be with him, his mate for life.

Rafe had driven up to the main house first. Mrs. Pidgeon had come to the door, all smiles, which kept catching him by surprise. She told him Ms. Alex had gone down to the Lodge. He drove back that way, parking in the shade of the beautiful orchid trees, the bauhinias. The front door, with its big bronze knocker, was open, so he walked into the cool of the High Victorian home Alex had decorated to her taste. It always amused him that, like "the den" at the mansion, the Lodge was bigger than the average house.

"Alex!" He didn't hide the joy of anticipation in his voice. This was the moment he had been waiting for all day. Better, he had good news for her. Their hit-and-run driver was just who they thought. What's more, he had confessed. "Alex?" he called again.

"I'll be there in a minute," she called back.

"In the studio?" He had high hopes she had been working. Alex was just so gifted. Gifts like that had to be used. "So what are you up to?" he asked, before he put a foot inside the large, light-filled studio with its views of the estate's gardens.

She was flushed, happy, her vivid blue eyes full of sparkle. But not *calm*. She reminded him of the little girl she had been, dying to tell him a secret. "I've been working all afternoon," she said, her posture somehow suggesting she mightn't let him in.

"That's great!" He strode around and then past her. The large room was filled with finished paintings stacked on the floor. A few hung on one wall. A watercolour of a jabiru stood on a medium-sized easel, and a long timber bench served as a worktable, covered in all the paraphernalia of the artist. One didn't expect to see a valuable Bokhara rug on an artist's floor nor the numerous objets d'art that filled a tall glass-fronted cabinet. But then Alex was an O'Farrell, with a breadth of culture one could only admire. Many times over the past years he had mourned the mis-mating of Rose Anne O'Farrell and Connor Ross. Connor might have come from a different planet than his highly refined wife, who was as delicate as a piece of porcelain.

"May I see?" His news about Ralston was moving out of his head.

"Well, I..."

He turned back to her. "Alex, I *can't* see. Why not?"

She gave an abrupt little laugh. "It was going to be a surprise, but I suppose..."

"Alex, darling, now you've got me mad keen to see it." The large easel she had been working on was turned away from him, but he walked straight to it, staring in amazement at a portrait of *himself*. Or himself in a different age. Eighteenth century? His initial reaction was intense pleasure mixed with a degree of shock. He took his time studying the painting—he thought the glimpse of the garden at one side of the canvas was a master stroke—then he looked back to where Alex was standing, a brilliant gleam in his eyes. "Alex, this is remarkable. It's *me* yet it's not me. It's a glorified me. I surely don't look as good as that."

She stared back at him gravely. "Yes, you do. I've caught you *precisely*. We only see ourselves in a mirror, Rafe. We don't see ourselves as other people see us."

He turned back to studying the portrait. "It's very dramatic. It looks like this guy is about to step out of the painting. Who am I supposed to be? One of my ancestors?"

"Not one of your ancestors. You. I simply borrowed the shirt and lengthened your hair." A memory flitted into her head. "You used to wear your hair quite long when you were at university."

"So I did. A lot of us did," he confirmed, beyond composing himself. He was intensely moved.

"You were a real heartbreaker." She smiled.

"*Were?*" he mocked, without turning away from the portrait. "This is extraordinarily well executed, Alex. I love it. It might be humble me, but it's a work of art. You ought to enter it for the Archibald Prize."

"I might, with your permission. It's *you* down to the last detail. Don't be so modest," she scoffed. "It's not finished, as you can see. There's quite a bit more to be done. But I have to say I was inspired. It's just possible I might even give it to you," she teased.

High emotion propelled Rafe swiftly around the long timber bench. He reached for her, folding his arms around her like in his dreams, burying his face in the halo of her beautiful hair.

"I am just so proud of you." He lifted his head to drop a short, intense kiss on her upturned mouth. "It would be a crime to keep you from your vocation. Life is our great gift, Alex, but life is short. You have to fly, my love. The pleasure and excitement you give to yourself when you're creating a painting, you can give to others who love and respect art."

She was excited, flushed, enraptured. "I *am* flying," she whispered. Her blue eyes had darkened to violet, exceptionally large as they always were at times of intense emotion. "You've always been loyal to me through all my stages. You've always supported me."

"Why wouldn't I?" He stared down into her face. "You're everything in the world to me, Alex. You're all around me wherever I go."

"That must be the definition of love," she said, tears welling in her eyes. "I wanted to be loved by you, Rafe, but my fears cost me." As she spoke, her legs were losing their strength. She felt she wouldn't be able to stand up without his arms tight around her.

"You're free now." Rafe bent his head to kiss her again. Longer. Deeper, their tongues executing a slow, ritualistic love dance. "God, before I forget everything!" Briefly he lifted his head before he lost all coherent thought. "Cliff Atkinson and I called in at Charlie Wilson's place. Guess who was there? Our friend Bob Ralston."

An immense sense of gratitude shot through her. "You caught him in the act?" she asked, linking her arms around his neck.

"In the act of inspecting the damage he had done," Rafe confirmed, equally elated they had caught the culprit.

"Did you ask him if he thought it was me driving the Merc?"

"He was drunk. He didn't intend to kill you," Rafe reported.

"Good Heavens, it's good to know he follows some ground rules."

"He wanted to give you a good fright."

"I'd say he gave us all a good fright." Alex found she could laugh. "Poor Amy, she's lucky she came out of it all with just a few bumps and bruises. I must tell her the culprit has been caught."

"A drunk driver, I think," Rafe suggested. "We don't want Mrs. Bateman flying back up here wanting to take on Ralston."

"One down, one to go," Alex said, in a voice full of thanks. "Next, we have to solve the enigma whose name currently is Sasha."

"Let's forget about Sasha for the time being, shall we?" Rafe suggested, holding the full length of her to his hard, aroused body. Her trembling was his trembling. It was as if they were melting into each other with every throb, every breath.

"No problem," Alex breathed into his open mouth. "Oh . . . you'll get paint on your clothes!"

"Then let's get them off, shall we?" Rafe kissed the velvety lids of her deep blue eyes. "You'd know better than I would how many famous painters made love in their studios."

"A great many without question, but you and I have the rest of the afternoon," she murmured, her body growing heavy with desire. The sensation was like shifting in and out of consciousness. Painting was a wonderful creative act. So was making love. Of far greater value was love's ability to make a child. She would not conceive today, but she had big plans for their future.

She felt Rafe lift her like a feather, carrying her down to the bedroom. She could deny him nothing. His will was her own. Whatever their future life was going to be, she knew, body and soul, she would give him the children they both yearned for. She saw that with a God-given super-clarity.

Two days later, when Alex was putting the finishing touches to her portrait of Rafe, she heard a car drive much too fast up past the Lodge, obviously on its way to the homestead. She recognised the sound of the engine. A Mercedes. It was Sasha. Had to be. The big walk-in wardrobe in her father's and Sasha's bedroom still held Sasha's vast array of expensive clothes. She would want to get them out of the house, as she had made it plain she wouldn't be returning. Mrs. Pidgeon wouldn't be there to greet her. The housekeeper had gone into town to replenish household supplies. Mrs. Pidgeon had made quite a hop, step, and jump these days. Alex had discovered the possible cause of her former grumpiness. Sasha had been paying the housekeeper a minimum wage. Mrs. Pidgeon, in no financial position to refuse, had been forced to accept it. When Alex found out, she'd doubled the housekeeper's wage, making no comment on, but deploring, Sasha's meanness.

Quickly she picked up a rag to wipe her hands, and then she made her way out of the studio to the front door, closing it behind her. Despite the heat, she sprinted along the drive, pounding over the lavender-blue carpet of spent jacaranda blossoms. Sasha retained her keys. She would let herself in. Alex didn't put it past her to lift a few valuable small items and stash them in whatever bag she had brought with her. Probably a large tote.

The day hadn't started well. She had just put down the phone to Amy, giving her the news about Bob Ralston's capture, when Max had rung, not sounding hopeful. Her father hadn't made a will with any of the firms that he and Todd Healey had judged high on the list. It looked very much like Connor Ross had died intestate. There was no news from their investigator, either.

"Early days, Alex. We really need the FBI on this one," said Max, sounding dispirited. "Healey will be going for a big settlement, so prepare yourself. Times have changed. It's a new world out there. Wills, where there is big money involved, are being contested every other day."

She already knew that from the media. Her friend Amy, being so canny, had early on arrived at the conclusion the hit-and-run driver had singled out Alex as his victim. Alex didn't keep the truth from her friend, but she was relieved when Amy told her she wasn't about to tell her mother. "Mum would be after his head on a plate."

No revelation!

Sasha's very expensive red Mercedes was parked a couple of feet from the foot of the stone steps. Probably she wanted a quick getaway. The front door was wide open. Alex walked in, calling, "Hello there, Sasha, it's me."

A moment later, Sasha appeared in the gallery, her upper body bent over the railing. "I need some of my things," she said in a don't-dare-to-stop-me tone of voice. "I'll have a removalist pick up the rest."

"You'll need a pantechnicon," Alex said wryly.

Sasha ignored that. "I want no trace of me left in this godforsaken house. It should be demolished, in my opinion. It's haunted."

Alex calmed the anger beating in her temples. "Haunted or not, it's one of the most beautiful colonial houses in the country. No demolition team would be allowed through the gates, Sasha. They would have to run over the entire population of the town. I understand from my solicitor this morning, an intensive check has been made, but it appears my father didn't make a will."

Sasha, on her signature high heels, teetered farther over the edge of the balustrade, slamming one hand down on it. "When I know all too well he *did* make one," she cried. "You *found* it. You saw he left everything to me, his wife, excluding you because he believed you had received quite enough from your mother and your grandparents, so you made the decision to destroy it."

"I wouldn't do a thing like that, Sasha, so dismiss the idea. I wouldn't have cared if my father did leave you everything he had left after you took him for a ride. The car, the clothes, the jewellery. You actually got away with a lot."

"Fancy you talking!" Sasha gave a harsh laugh. "You're *rich*." She sneered, "On account of your family. *You* didn't make the money. Your bloody people did. What about the money they made in the gold rush! Think about that." She gave another knowing smirk. "I'm talking spite here, *Sandy*. You hate me. You look down your nose at me just like your uppity grandparents treated Connor with contempt. I told Todd how you attacked me. Went for my throat like a harpy. I told him behind that so-ladylike manner you have a violent temper."

"Wouldn't it have been wiser then, not to come alone?" Alex asked.

Sasha stood away from the rail. "If anything happens to me, the authorities will know who to blame," she warned.

"Wow, then I'd better be careful. Did you bother to tell Mr. Healey the hateful things you had to say about me?" Alex started to mount the stairs.

"I'm warning you, Sandy." Sasha's body language said she was genuinely anxious about what Alex might do.

"Sasha, you're quite safe," Alex told her when she reached the top of the staircase. "Get your things. Would you like a hand?"

"Never from you." Sasha turned away.

"Did your lawyer tell you my father had consulted a divorce lawyer?" Alex asked to her stepmother's back. She was finding Sasha's manner unusual for a woman who had received such a devastating piece of news.

Sasha spun about, a tinge of alarm injected into her voice. "Oh yeah? When was this?"

"He didn't tell you then?" Alex said. "I wonder why? I have to say I'm very surprised Todd Healey hasn't passed on that vital piece of information to you, his client."

"Todd's in Sydney," Sasha said sharply, as though that explained everything.

"The law firm my father consulted is in Sydney," Alex told her. "Do you suppose Mr. Healey set up a meeting with them?"

Sasha held up a forefinger. She began to shake it violently at Alex. "Don't you dare lie to me, you bitch. There was never a cross word between Connor and me. He was *mad* about me."

"Mad about something you had done, more like it," Alex said. "Something he found out about, perhaps?"

"He found out absolutely *nothing*!" Sasha shouted, temper flashing. "My past is an open book."

"Is it?" Alex asked. "Are you sure about that?"

Sasha didn't answer. She swung about, continuing on her way to the bedroom she had shared with her late, if not loving, husband.

It appeared it hadn't taken her father all that long to realize he had dug himself in deeper than he had ever intended, Alex thought. For a moment there she had almost given in to the temptation to ask Sasha about the postcard. But then Sasha could avoid answering or deny all knowledge of it. Before one could accuse anyone of anything there had to be proof. No proof was as yet forthcoming.

Alex went back down the stairs to the kitchen. She would make herself a cup of coffee. She had told Mrs. Pidgeon not to hurry. The housekeeper could spend a little more time in town, enjoying a lunch break. There were two excellent coffee shops on the main street.

The spotless kitchen was what a real estate agent could well describe as a state-of-the-art country kitchen with all the modern conveniences. The big walk-in pantry was in splendid order as well. Method was everywhere. Mrs. Pidgeon was worth every penny of her wages. She was a very good cook too, if not adventurous, but no one could fault her baking.

Alex studied a large black-and-white framed photo on the wall, of a beaming Mrs. Pidgeon and a smiling former lady mayor. In it the mayor was holding up a large caption that read, First Prize Rich Fruit Cake. It was good for someone to excel at something, Alex thought. Mrs. Pidgeon was definitely happier these days. Alex saw keeping all of Lavender Hill's staff happy as part of her job. It was a policy that had good outcomes for all.

An hour later and Sasha still hadn't sorted out her things. Alex went quietly back up the stairs. She really wanted to know what Sasha was doing. The door to her mother's bedroom was ajar. She hadn't left it like that; the door had been shut. She waited a moment, and then she moved down the hallway, pausing outside the bedroom before pushing back the door. Inside, Sasha, caught by surprise, slammed shut the lid of the marriage chest at the foot of the bed. It was clear she had been rifling through the contents.

"What exactly do you think you're doing?" Alex fired off. "You have no business in here, Sasha. I'd like you to get out. Right away."

Sasha stood her ground, a strangely jubilant look in her eyes. "Connor told me there were secret places in this house to stash things. I just thought I'd take a peek around this room. The chest seemed a likely place to keep one's valuables, though I suppose it's too easy to get at. Who used to sleep here, Marie Antoinette? You see how outdated it all is?" She stared around her at the Old World opulence.

"I'm sure you wouldn't like me to attack you a second time," Alex said, making a decisive move towards the older woman.

"No need." Sasha waved a hand. "I'm going. How many other people know about the secret hiding places?"

"I suppose you're talking about the jewellery?"

Sasha smiled almost happily. "We're going to take you for all we can get, *Sandy*. I don't believe for a moment Connor wanted to divorce me. Normally couples get into huge fights before they decide to divorce. Connor and I never had a cross word."

Which just could be true. "My father didn't show his feelings, Sasha," Alex explained. "That blinded you. I'm afraid you vastly overestimated your hold on him. Worse, I think he found out something about you that worried him badly," she said, watching Sasha gravely.

"Nonsense!" Sasha looked entirely secure. "Believe me, Connor would have remained faithful to me. All you're doing—all you have ever done—is insult me. All the schemes you and your solicitor—who is no match for Todd, even you must be able to see that—have thought up will be knocked down. We'll have our day in court, *Sandy*. I'll get what I'm due, plus what Connor was due. You've always hated the fact I became equal with you."

"Why not be superior, while you're at it? Leave, please, Sasha. I'm surprised you dared to enter this room. Ghosts, remember?"

"I don't believe in ghosts."

"We all believe in ghosts. They are around in some form or other."

* * *

Sometime later, Sasha emerged from her former bedroom holding only one small Louis Vuitton suitcase. "I'd appreciate it if you didn't go inside," she said to Alex in a lofty tone of voice.

"You have my word. I have no interest in your things, Sasha. Let me know what time and what day your removalist is coming."

"This will all become public, you know," Sasha said as they made their way down the hallway to the top of the staircase.

"I don't know what you mean," Alex said. "The whole town pretty much knows the sad story. You didn't win any accolades not going to the hospital. Even more damning was not attending your husband's funeral."

"I was too upset." A dogged look came over Sasha's face.

"It didn't seem that way when you turned up at the wake. You married my father because you thought he was a rich man. We all know that."

Sasha gave a tight smile. "You're frightened of me and what we're set to grab off you."

Wise or not, Alex spoke with a mild tone of contempt. "No, I'm not, *Lucy*."

In front of her eyes, Sasha's expression turned explosive. It was as if a bomb had been detonated inside her. Too many bad memories there, Alex thought. Too much left behind. Too much to hide. Sasha *was* Lucy. That was the only explanation for her violent reaction.

Sasha dropped the suitcase she had been carrying, allowing it to tumble all the way down the stairs. "*What* did you call me?"

She had to finish what she had started. "Lucy," Alex repeated. "Lucy-Lu. That *is* your real name, isn't it?"

Sasha clasped the palms of her hands to her ears. "You're mad!" she cried, shaking her head in violent denial. "You're a liar. A wicked liar." There was a deep red flush of humiliation on her face.

"I don't think so." It wasn't until that moment Alex had an inkling how unloved Sasha/Lucy might have been in her life. "In fact, I'm sure I'm right. There is so much to learn about you. Probably a lot no one would approve of."

In other parts of the estate there was movement everywhere, workers going to and fro. Inside the Lavender Hills mansion all was hushed, but full of danger. Sasha's body had fallen into an odd pose. It reminded Alex of a viper about to strike. That alone should have given her warning. Sasha had flattened her lower back against the wrought iron railing; her blond head, though held high, was inclined sharply forward.

Shaking inside, still Alex ploughed on, now that she had found an opening. "We're investigating further, Lucy. Information about you will come to light. There had to be a reason Dad went to a divorce lawyer. He had learned something damning about you. Something he couldn't condone."

Sasha looked back at the younger woman with wild eyes. Then she leapt into motion. She struck out with all her might at Alex, fully intending to send her careening down the stairs. Her small hands were thrust unbelievably hard against Alex's shoulders. They had the strength of primitive fear. Sasha might have been fighting for her life, so intent was she on overcoming Alex's defence. Her light blue eyes were wide open, yet their expression was strangely blank, almost glassy. Alex, taller, stronger, fitter, flung herself sideways, making it difficult for Sasha to keep her grip on her.

"Stop. Stop *now*!" she shouted. "Stop, Sasha, before we both fall down the stairs."

Instead Sasha continued to thrash out, her desire to send Alex crashing down onto the floor of the entrance hall overcoming every other consideration. Alex stumbled on a stair. Her heart rocked and a stab of pain shot up her leg. She made a frantic grab for the wrought-iron railing and held on to it as hard as she could, though a small scroll was digging into her palm. Even then, Sasha reached for her. It was as if she wanted to claw Alex's eyes out.

Instead it was Sasha in her high heels who couldn't keep herself upright. She lost her footing and with a panic-stricken cry went tumbling down the stairs, landing on the parqueted floor like a half-filled sack.

God!

It was a heart-stopping moment. Alex stood in place, gasping as though it was she who had toppled down the stairs. It took a moment more to stabilize herself. Her heart was pounding painfully against her rib cage. She stared down at Sasha. She lay sprawled faceup, half on her side. Her slender legs were splayed. One of her arms was bent at an odd angle. Obviously she had fallen on it. Was it broken? No blood, thank God. Sasha was moaning as if terribly hurt.

Alex's immediate response was to help. With clenched teeth she rushed down the stairs, startled as Mrs. Pidgeon, back from her shopping trip, bustled into the entrance hall, looking very shaken up.

"Call an ambulance, would you?" Alex called to her urgently. "Mrs. Ross has slipped and fallen down the stairs."

Tears of pain were running down Sasha's face, the tears blackened by the runoff from her mascara. "You pushed me," she gasped, trying to raise her head. "You bloody well pushed me. You'll pay for it. It's a miracle you didn't kill me."

Alex didn't waste any time denying the accusation. Sasha was bound to repeat it endlessly, to the police and anyone who would listen. Mrs. Pidgeon wasn't about to waste time either. She turned away without hesitation. "I'll ring for the ambulance, Ms. Alex. It looks as though the arm might be broken. Maybe not."

What to do? Sasha was fully conscious, though her skin looked clammy. "Let me make you more comfortable," Alex implored. "I think I should apply a splint to your arm."

"Don't come near me," Sasha panted, like a woman in genuine fear of her life.

"At least let me put a cushion under your head and your feet."

"Get away," Sasha cried hoarsely, the effort sending her into a dizzy spin.

Whether Sasha wanted it or not, Alex found two cushions to raise Sasha's head and her feet. Sasha really should have been turned more on her side in case she started to vomit, but Alex was loath to touch her in case she did the wrong thing.

It seemed like an eternity, yet it was only eight minutes before the ambulance swept up the drive. Alex was moved gently aside as the paramedics knelt to assess Sasha's injuries. "The arm isn't broken, I'm fairly sure," the older man said. "She'll need an X-ray to be certain. I'd say she's badly sprained her arm and wrist. Good thing the floor is wooden and not marble."

"Did you hear a snap, Mrs. Ross?" the other paramedic asked, well aware of the identity of the patient.

"Hadn't you better get me to hospital instead of asking stupid questions?" Sasha snapped.

The older paramedic's eyes locked on his partner's.

"She bloody well pushed me down the stairs." Sasha dug up enough strength to pass on the accusation. "She could have killed me."

Alex spoke calmly, even though her insides were churning. "Not true, gentlemen. Mrs. Ross fell. The high heels didn't help."

"Right! We'll get her to hospital for an X-ray. You'll follow, Ms. Ross?"

"Don't let her near me," Sasha cried, clearly in pain, although some of her colour was returning. "You have to protect me."

"I'll follow on," said Alex. "I need to be sure she's okay."

"I'll have you up on a charge. I mean it, *Sandy*." Sasha, using up all the oxygen in her lungs, was being lifted very carefully onto a stretcher.

Mrs. Pidgeon, who had been standing as invisible as a shadow, stepped forward, suddenly speaking up. "It was your own doing, madam." She addressed Sasha. "I heard Ms. Alex cry out, "'Stop. Stop now, Sasha, before we both fall down the stairs.'"

"Liar! You're on her side every step of the way. You'd say anything to keep your job." Sasha glared at the housekeeper. "I think the police will find my version the one to believe."

Mrs. Pidgeon stared back at Sasha with a mixture of pity and hostility. "I wouldn't put my money on it."

Alex was at the hospital, with Max on hand, when Rafe finally arrived. He had received a private call advising him of the situation. He strode up to both of them, clearly angry, upset, and on edge. "These charges will never be brought, will they, Max?" he asked, putting a protective arm around Alex's waist.

"Mrs. Ross seems to think she's in a very powerful position," Max explained. "Todd Healey is in Sydney at the moment, but he has been advised. He'll be returning on an afternoon flight."

"So what was he doing in Sydney?" Rafe asked.

"I would say meeting up with the divorce lawyer Connor consulted," Max replied.

"So what happened?" Rafe stared down into Alex's strained face.

"My fault," she said with a near despairing sigh. "I was fool enough to call her Lucy."

"No!" Rafe groaned.

Alex kept her head down. "Okay, I admit it, I provoked her."

"I don't give a damn about your provoking her," Rafe said tautly, "so long as I or Max was there to protect you. You put yourself in harm's way. That's a hard, cold fact."

"Don't I know it," Alex exclaimed, pulling away from him. "Don't lecture me, Rafe."

"Please, let's settle down," Max implored, a kind of desperation in his own voice.

Rafe was keen to start up again. "Alex put herself in a potentially dangerous position and I'm supposed to feel settled about it? So she got hysterical. Is that what you're saying, Alex?"

"That's what I'm saying, *Rafe*." She had never been great at keeping her temper with him.

"Go through it," Rafe said, well used to their clashes.

"Sasha arrived wanting to pack a few things," she said patiently. "Of course I agreed. She was taking her time, so I went upstairs, only to find her in the master bedroom. She was rifling through the marriage chest at the end of the bed."

"*Was* she!" Rafe said in a deep, dark voice.

"I expected her to be embarrassed at the very least, but she appeared quite confident. She would have been searching for the jewellery collection. She seems to have a thing about jewellery. Actually, she was acting as if she were entitled to half of it."

"So how did you make it to the stairs?" he asked, visualizing the scene.

"She wanted to get out of the house as quickly as possible. I escorted her along the hallway. It was when we reached the top of the staircase that she told me I was terrified of how much she was going to grab from the estate. It was then that I called her *Lucy*."

"I might have guessed you would." Rafe gave another low groan. "She must have gone ballistic?"

"Pretty much," Alex answered wryly. "She tossed her suitcase down the stairs, then she attempted to toss me. For a little woman she's amazingly strong."

"Fear is a pretty powerful incentive," Rafe said.

Max lowered his head, supporting his chin with his hand. He was filled with horror for Sasha and admiration for Alex, even if she had taken a calculated risk.

"I'm taller and fitter, so I was able to fend her off. Plus the fact she was wearing her signature spike heels," Alex was saying.

"You're okay?"

"Brilliant! Thanks for asking," Alex told him pointedly, her vivid blue eyes sparkling.

Rafe reached out, drawing her back to him. "Whoo... you're angry. Settle down. I know you've had a bad experience. You might consider that so have I. The bloody woman attacked you."

"She is Lucy. Lucy-Lu," Alex answered, mollified. "Of that we can be certain."

"I don't know that we can prove it," said Max. "The police have far better resources than anyone else. We should tell them everything. I've seen many lives ruined by lies. Mrs. Ross has accused Alex of pushing her down the stairs."

"I know that. It was Cliff Atkinson who rang me," Rafe said. "I also know Mrs. Pidgeon was there. She backed you, Alex, but Sasha is claiming self-interest on the housekeeper's part, that she just said what she did to hold on to her job."

"So it's my word and Mrs. Pidgeon's word against the word of a truly bizarre woman. Speaking of which, what are we going to do with her? We can't just abandon her. We'll know shortly if she's broken her arm or not. Even if she hasn't, the arm must be badly sprained. The wrist as well. She's got no one to come to her aid."

"What about Patty, her best friend?" Rafe asked with a lick of sarcasm. "Of course there's nothing else for it but to make sure she's looked after. It can be arranged. What about you and Valerie, Max?" he asked, tongue in cheek.

"Stop it, Rafe," Alex said. "He's teasing, Max. He's good at that."

"She'd move in like a shot with you, Rafe," Max returned, hiding a grin.

"A man is supposed to be safe in his own home," Rafe said. "It's all very odd, isn't it? Sasha has obviously changed her name. There was a reason. The postcard had to have come in an envelope, and had to have been lying around someplace; Connor must have found the postcard in its envelope. It would have had Lucy-Lu's address on it. Connor for some reason decides to check it out. He already mistrusts Sasha. He would have noted Sasha's Kiwi accent occasionally coming to the fore, just as we did."

Alex frowned. "Dad would have held on to the envelope, wouldn't you say?"

"That's a yes." Both men agreed.

"I haven't had the heart to go through his clothes. My poor father! He could have shoved the envelope in a pocket while he read the postcard. He wouldn't have shown it to Sasha, having learned she was a pathological liar. Proof is, she didn't know a thing about it. She was stunned out of her mind when I called her *Lucy*—" Alex broke off.

All three heads turned. A nurse was wheeling Sasha towards them. The white-coated radiologist was walking alongside. Sasha's arm was in a sling. They could see a compression bandage on her wrist, which was held higher than her heart, but as yet no sign of plaster on her arm. Sasha looked like she had put in a very long day, as well she might.

"Rafe!" Sasha called out, as if there were indeed a merciful God.

"I don't believe this," Rafe muttered. "Could someone please tell *Lucy* I'm not her pal?"

"You should have told her ages ago," said Alex tartly.

He gave her a sharp smile. "You think she would have understood?"

"Possibly not."

"I'll do the talking."

"That's nothing new." Alex gave him her best smile.

"I'm your man, Alex," he reminded her.

Whatever his feelings, Rafe greeted Sasha courteously, asking her how she felt and about her condition.

The radiologist filled them in. "I'm pleased to tell you neither the arm nor the wrist was broken. Minor damage to the ligaments. Mrs. Ross was lucky. The sprains will heal on their own. She needs rest. An anti-inflammatory drug will help manage the pain and the inflammation. You're here to take care of her?" he asked hopefully. Mrs. Ross had certainly not charmed the pants off him. She needed some serious work on her social skills.

"We are," said Rafe, putting the doctor's mind at rest.

Sasha's smug expression said that was very much what she had expected.

A lengthy palm-lined drive, then the house. Jabiru Plantation's homestead was a large, modern sanctuary in cyclone country. Rafe and Alex's friends, Jon and Miranda Moore, were standing at the front door. As soon as Rafe pulled up, they walked out onto the drive to meet them.

"Who are these people, Rafe?" Sasha demanded with a flash of disapproval.

"Good friends of mine, Sasha," Rafe said, already opening the door of the Range Rover. "Bless them, they've offered to help out."

Sasha spluttered. She had thought she would have Rafe to herself. After all, he had dropped off Connor's dreadful daughter at Lavender Hill. She could never go back to that place. It would be like a plunge into hell for her.

"Jon and Miranda are very capable," Rafe told her smoothly, opening her door. "They'll get you settled in. Look after your every need. As always, I have work to do."

"You'll be back this evening?" Sasha asked, a little wildly. She didn't have a clue about these people. Probably they were just like the rest of the townspeople. She had taken an ill-deserved hammering from them.

"Of course," Rafe assured her.

"I don't want anyone else," said Sasha, blind to what she didn't want to see. It had always been that way with her.

Sasha had had the use of the large walk-in wardrobe, still packed to the rafters with clothes and a collection of shoes Imelda Marcos might have coveted. Connor had had to make do with a mirror-fronted wardrobe and twin chests of drawers.

Rafe and Alex stood outside the bedroom door. "You're not coming in?" he asked.

"No. I'm not." Alex didn't feel up to the task of going through her father's things.

"That's okay. I don't expect you to." Rafe pulled her near. His long fingers tenderly stroked her face, before he bent to kiss her with the deep need that was in him. "Go downstairs, my love, and say lots of prayers."

"My prayers haven't helped much in the past," said the bereft Alex.

"Remember what your parish priest said at your father's funeral?" Rafe asked her quietly. "'Even when you think you've lost your faith in God, keep praying to Him like you still have it.' I think that would work. Never give up hope, Alex. When hope comes to an end, so do we. Our life has already made a glorious turnaround. We have each other for as long as we both shall live. That's all the hope *I* need. I love you with all my heart."

"As I love you," Alex declared without pause.

"Anyway, it's entirely possible Connor might have learned something from your mother," he added in a gently mocking tone. "She never threw anything out."

Even feeling as she did, Alex had to laugh. "The O'Farrells were well-known hoarders."

"Certainly not of junk," said a sardonic Rafe.

After Alex had gone he shut the door and walked to the first of a pair of lacquered walnut dressers. He didn't want to search through Connor's things. It seemed like a huge invasion of privacy, even though the man was dead. No one could have said Connor was tidy, he thought as he opened the first drawer stuffed with clean but rumpled t-shirts. No attempt had been made to fold them. Clearly Sasha hadn't done the wifely thing, keeping her husband's things in order. Neither had she instructed her housekeeper to do so. Perhaps she herself had made the mess, looking for something. Half groaning to himself, he began his search. A proper search it had to be. It would be extremely difficult to find answers.

It took him a while to thoroughly examine the contents of the first dresser. Nothing! He braced himself to search the second dresser. He wouldn't have described himself as a religious man, yet he had the feeling he was being *helped*. The Ross family was really his family, too. He had mourned over Kelvin's body, even as he held the young, weeping Alex in his arms. He had mourned over Rose Anne, who had always greeted him with the loveliest smiles, even when she was dying. He knew the truth about Connor, his failure to support his wife and daughter, yet Connor had been kind enough to him. Something momentous had happened to Connor that had rocked him to the realization that his second marriage was a disaster.

Moments later, all their prayers appeared to be answered.

"Hallelujah!" Spontaneously he burst into the joyous exclamation.

Tucked away in a pair of old socks that really should have been thrown away, he found what he was looking for. A crumpled-up envelope. It bore a Lucy Bingle's New Zealand address, a small town in the South Island, the stamp impressed with the date June 17, 1998. It was all they needed to track down Sasha, alias Lucy Bingle. Here was the final link. Sasha had been hiding a secret so serious she had lashed out violently at Alex, hardly caring she might have killed her pushing her down the stairs.

Even afterwards she had shown no remorse or shame. Instead she had tried to place the guilt at Alex's door. Sasha actually deserved what was coming to her. Even so, he felt pity. Lucy Bingle's history, he felt certain, was not a good one. It hardly seemed appropriate to unmask her, at least until she had recovered from her injuries, which thank God were nowhere near as serious as they could have been.

Further investigations got underway the same day. It took another four days before all the facts were in, due to the far-reaching resources of the police. Bingle was not Sasha's surname. Bingle was her *married* name.

Lucy Hobson had been married at age seventeen to a young man from her hometown, a Danny Bingle. After Bingle discovered Lucy was not pregnant as she had claimed, he left her, joining the New Zealand army. He had never sought a divorce. Neither had Lucy. Bingle had a partner of many years long-standing. A male. A fellow soldier. Lucy, reborn in her early thirties as Sasha Stevens, had nearly ten years later entered into a bigamous marriage with Connor Ross, thinking her past would never come to light. Patty, Patricia Moffat, had been Lucy's close friend from childhood. Patricia Moffat had died in a skiing accident at age twenty-six.

On the face of it, it seemed like an incredible deception. Had Sasha proved to be a loving wife and companion to Alex's father, the deception might never have been discovered. Sasha had underestimated everyone, especially the man with whom she had entered into a bigamous relationship.

Alex deplored the sickening shock her father would have received when he found out the truth about the woman he had married in good faith. Everyone was conscious of the fact that Connor had never confronted her nor revealed her crime, punishable by law.

Small wonder her father had been acting so oddly in his last days, Alex thought. Small wonder he let the quad bike run away with him. It might have had a connection to his desire to run away from the terrible mistake he had made. Alex couldn't bear to spend any time pondering that. Sadly, her father had taken stock on his own. He never had confided in her. That was her punishment for outliving Kelvin. He had visited a divorce lawyer in Sydney. It was a one-off visit, but as they had found out, he hadn't revealed the fact that he had unwittingly entered into a bigamous marriage. That would have been too much of an assault on his pride.

The police and the two lawyers representing Alex and Sasha were told everything. The whole mess was revealed, on the record. Todd Healey had not appeared unduly shocked. No doubt he was thinking he could represent Sasha on her bigamy charge. The penalty was five years' imprisonment. Bigamy was a very serious charge. The time was rapidly approaching when Sasha had to be told about their investigations and what they had uncovered.

In the meantime, the problem of Sasha Ross remained. Alex wondered what she might do when she had to face the consequences of her actions. For all the wrongs Sasha had inflicted on her father—and her, for that matter—she couldn't bear the thought of sending Sasha, another woman, to jail. It was an extremely unhappy situation.

Sasha remained at Rafe's home, as if he were responsible for her and her well-being. Rafe was the only person she would talk to, put in the unenviable position of judging the day Sasha would be strong enough to face the charges that would be brought against her.

Sasha Ross was an imposter. Sasha Ross was Lucy Bingle. She had brought shame on herself and shame on a fine family. Rafe had been asked to be there when Lucy Bingle was confronted. He had agreed, providing Alex was by his side.

Sasha's face lit up when Rafe, after knocking, entered the large, very comfortable room she had been given during her stay.

"Oh, Rafe, how lovely you're home," she cried eagerly. It was a glimpse into the mind of a woman who had never found a man to love her, nor she him.

"I've brought Alex with me," Rafe said, watching Sasha's expression turn, as expected, to fury.

"What?" she cried loudly, one hand clinging hard to the side of her armchair.

"Good morning," Alex said quietly as she followed Rafe into the room.

"God Almighty, Rafe!" Sasha cried, half rising. "Whyever would you spring this woman on me? I never want to see her again. She's responsible for pushing me down the stairs. She should have been taken to account and charged. Tell me she has been. I don't want to hear any apology from her," she declared stoutly. "It will never be accepted."

"No apology, *Lucy*," Alex said in the same quiet tone. "Believe it or not I *am* sorry, but this isn't going to be a good day for you. It has all come to an end." She turned her head, gesturing with her hand to someone standing outside the open door. "The police are here to talk to you."

"*What?*" Lucy Bingle fell back, her pretty face losing all colour.

Sergeant Clifford Atkinson stepped into the room followed by his constable. The life history of Lucy Bingle, née Hobson, was about to emerge. Against all odds, everyone involved felt sorry for her. Todd Healey was on hand to give legal advice. Alex had already informed him his costs would be covered.

The facts were read out by Sergeant Atkinson in a controlled voice: Lucy Hobson had entered into a legal marriage at age seventeen when she was hardly more than a child. She had received little in the way of a formal education. She had come from an unhappy home where her father was abusive to his wife and children. What Lucy had going for her was her prettiness. But her overt sexuality had worked against her. She had claimed she was pregnant at the time of her legal marriage to a young man barely two years her senior.

Lucy Bingle, née Hobson, had probably not thought it a serious matter when she had entered into a bigamous marriage some twenty-five years later. Lack of understanding of the law, however, was no excuse. At the same time, no one had any doubt her very experienced lawyer, or someone in his firm, would successfully defend Lucy Bingle against the maximum penalty of jail.

Many extenuating circumstances would be found to get Lucy Bingle off the hook. In her favour was the fact she was being supported by the daughter of the man with whom she had entered into a bigamous relationship. Lucy Bingle made a statement clearing Connor Ross, her bigamous husband, of complicity. Connor Ross had never known of her deception.

Alex and Rafe decided to keep it that way. The usual bush telegraph got underway. It looked like the nightmare was over. The pretentious Mrs. Connor Ross had begun mucking up her life early, it seemed. Apparently she had never stopped.

Epilogue

Four months later

It was the morning of the wedding of Alexandra Ross to Raphael Rutherford. The whole town had sprung to life. There wasn't a soul who upon waking didn't feel a surge of joy. Not everyone could fit into the bride's parish church, St. Anthony's—it was way too small—but the crowd of well-wishers could await the appearance of the bridal party on the street and the freshly manicured grounds outside. Besides, guests aside, who would attend a private reception in the homestead, it hardly mattered. The whole town had been invited to a barbecue on Lavender Hill's splendid grounds. Celebrations were expected to go on into the night.

The tragic years were all but forgotten. The woman who had had the gall to call herself Mrs. Connor Ross was back in New Zealand. She had escaped jail time. *How* was none too clear, but it was rumoured Alexandra had helped her by giving the woman a settlement. Would mysteries never cease!

The bride had three lovely bridesmaids to attend her. Her chief bridesmaid was her friend Amy Bateman, who had bounced back from her accident. The wedding party also included a page boy and two little flower girls, the elder, seven, to keep the exuberant little ones in check. The bride was to be given away by the Ross family's great friend, their solicitor, Max Hoffmann. What the bride's party would be wearing had been kept a very closely guarded secret. The bridegroom would be attended by his best man and two groomsmen.

A lot had happened in the past months. Lavender Hill homestead, where the married couple would be living, had been extensively refurbished and many possessions of value auctioned off by Christie's in Sydney. The proceeds had been used to upgrade facilities around the town. A splendid three-tier fountain was installed in the town park, where the play area for the children had been refurbished, to everyone's delight. Even the local kindergarten had greatly benefited.

The whole town could begin again. Rafe Rutherford had sold off Jabiru Macadamia Plantation to his best man, Jonathon Moore, and his family. Everyone knew Rafe had stacks of interests. He and partners were developing a small island off the glorious Whitsundays as a holiday resort. All were important events: important for the newly married Rutherfords, important for the town and the state.

Alex walked down the aisle on Max's arm to join her beloved Rafe. She wore a beautiful white chiffon and lace wedding gown, the strapless bodice moulded tight to her body, the long chiffon skirt flowing. She felt like a princess who had been released from her ivory tower by her prince. Swinging from her ears were the O'Farrell diamond and sapphire drop earrings. Dipping into her creamy cleavage, the matching O'Farrell diamond and sapphire necklace. It had been quite a job for Rafe to match the splendour of the precious O'Farrell Burmese sapphires for Alex's engagement ring, but match them his jeweller did, sourcing the intensely violet-blue four-carat central stone from Sri Lanka.

Alex's bridesmaids, walking gracefully behind her, wore short lavender-blue dresses with wonderful full, ruffled skirts and tight-fitting, strapless bodices. High-heeled gold sandals adorned their feet. Around their necks they wore stunning gold and amethyst pendant necklaces, gifts from the groom. Alex didn't wear a veil. She had opted for a coronet of handcrafted silk roses mixed with shimmering crystals and tiny pearls. It sat on her long unbound hair, resting on her forehead. Her bridesmaids wore the same exquisite headdresses. All carried bouquets of white flowers and Thai orchids. The little flower girls were dressed in pink silk with pink and lilac ribbons in their hair. The page boy had consented to a white pleated silk shirt over *long* white pants. Those long pants had thrilled him.

Rafe was well represented by friends and family alike. His mother and his married sister and her husband had flown from London for the happy occasion, all dressed to the nines. Rafe and his attendants looked swooningly handsome in especially tailored dark grey morning suits with pale lavender vests over pristine white dress shirts, with blue, pink and lavender paisley silk ties. This was a once-in-a-lifetime occasion no one would be likely to forget.

The beauty of the bride, her radiance and her expression of great happiness, touched every heart. Some closest to the family had the feeling Alex's mother and father and her forever-young brother were at peace and had given them special permission to attend Alexandra's wedding to a man everyone heartily admired and approved of. The ladies who looked after the church had done a wonderful job of decorating it for the wedding. The altar looked resplendent. The pews were tied with perfectly arranged big, wide white taffeta ribbons. Everyone felt the joy. That joy brought forth many a time-honoured tear.

Alex handed her beautiful bouquet to Amy, who smilingly took it. Max then placed Alex's hand in that of her waiting bridegroom. Rafe's dark eyes were brilliant with emotion. No mistaking his love for his bride, or her love for him. This was a marriage ordained in Heaven. The "Wedding March" on the organ faded away. The parish priest stood ready to perform the marriage ceremony. At last, at *long* last, Alex and Rafe were to become husband and wife and move into Lavender Hill together. The little humming sounds, the little chokes of emotion that could be heard throughout the congregation, fell silent.

The parish priest in his special wedding vestments moved forward to address bride and groom, calling for the exchange of vows that was at the heart of the sacrament of marriage. Bride and groom had memorized their vows, both speaking clearly. Both, with joined hands, promised before God to be true to one another, in good times and bad, in sickness and in health, to love and honour one another all the days of their lives until death do they part. The light through the stained-glass arched windows spilled every colour of the rainbow over the couple, the colours almost impossibly bright but never blinding. It was a light so lovely, so blessed, row after row of the congregation found themselves rising to their feet. The small country church was filled with a sense of wonder. Most had been in and out of the church countless times, but none had seen that particular radiance. There was a hush as Rafe took his bride in his arms to give her his ceremonial kiss, his tribute to his new wife.

Bride and groom turned, facing their wedding guests. Their faces were shining with joy. The organist, a fine musician who had spent many hours practising for the big day, broke into Mozart's "Exsultate, Jubilate" as bride and groom commenced their slow walk down the aisle. Every face turned to them appeared a little dazed but truly happy. When bride and groom reached the door of the church, the street and the church grounds resounded with cheers and loud applause.

Nothing like a so obviously blessed wedding to bring people together.

Let the banquet begin.

Please turn the page for an exciting peek at
Poinciana Road
by
Margaret Way!
Available in November 2016 at
your favourite bookstores and e-tailers.

Chapter 1

Mallory knew the route to Forrester Base Hospital as well as she knew the lines on the palms of her hands. She had never had the dubious pleasure of having her palm read, but she had often wondered whether palmistry was no more than superstition, or if there was something to it. Her life line showed a catastrophic break, and one had actually occurred. If she read beyond the break, she was set to receive a card from the Queen when she turned one hundred. As it was, she was twenty-eight. There was plenty of time to get her life in order and find some happiness. Currently her life was largely devoted to work. She allowed herself precious little free time. It was a deliberate strategy. Keep on the move. Don't sit pondering over what was lodged in the soul.

The driver of the little Mazda ahead was starting to annoy her. He was showing excessive respect for the speed limit, flashing his brake lights at every bend in the road. She figured it was time to pass, and was surprised when the driver gave her a loud honk for no discernible reason. She held up her hand, waved. A nice little gesture of camaraderie and goodwill.

She was almost there, thank the Lord. The farther she had travelled from the state capital, Brisbane, the more the drag on her emotions. That pesky old drag would never go away. It was a side effect of the baggage she carted around and couldn't unload. It wasn't that she didn't visualize a brave new world. It was just that so far it hadn't happened. Life was neither kind nor reasonable. She knew that better than most. She also knew one had to fight the good fight even when the chances of getting knocked down on a regular basis were high.

It had been six years and more since she had been back to her hometown. She wouldn't be returning now, she acknowledged with a stab of guilt, except for the unexpected heart attack of her uncle Robert. Her uncle, a cultured, courtly man, had reared her from age seven. No one else had been offering. Certainly not her absentee father, or her maternal grandparents, who spent their days cruising the world on the *Queen Mary 2*. True, they did call in to see her whenever they set foot on dry land, bearing loads of expensive gifts. But sadly they were unable to introduce a child into their busy lives. She was the main beneficiary of their will. They had assured her of that; a little something by way of compensation. She was, after all, their only grandchild. It was just at seven, she hadn't fit into their lifestyle. Decades later she still didn't.

Was it any wonder she loved her Uncle Robert? He was her superhero. Handsome, charming, well off. A bachelor by choice. Her dead mother, Claudia, had captured his heart long ago when they were young and deeply in love. Her mother had gone to her grave with her uncle's heart still pocketed away. It was an extraordinary thing and in many ways a calamity, because Uncle Robert had never considered snatching his life back. He was a lost cause in the marriage stakes. As was she, for that matter.

To fund what appeared on the surface to be a glamorous lifestyle, Robert James had quit law to become a very popular author of novels of crime and intrigue. The drawing card for his legions of fans was his comedic detective, Peter Zero, never as famous as the legendary Hercule Poirot, but much loved by the readership.

Pulp fiction, her father, Nigel James, Professor of English and Cultural Studies at Melbourne University, called it. Her father had always stomped on his older brother's talent. "Fodder for the ignorant masses to be read on the train." Her father never minced words, the crueller the better. To put a name to it, her father was an all-out bastard.

It was Uncle Robert who had spelled love and a safe haven to her. He had taken her to live with him at Moonglade, his tropical hideaway in far North Queensland. In the infamous "blackbirding" days, when South Sea islanders had been kidnapped to work the Queensland cane fields, Moonglade had been a thriving sugar plantation. The house had been built by one Captain George Rankin, who had at least fed his workers bananas, mangoes, and the like and paid them a token sum to work in a sizzling hot sun like the slaves they were.

Uncle Robert had not bought the property as a working plantation. Moonglade was his secure retreat from the world. He could not have chosen a more idyllic spot, with two listed World Heritage areas on his doorstep: the magnificent Daintree Rainforest, the oldest living rainforest on the planet, and the glorious Great Barrier Reef, the world's largest reef system.

His heart attack had come right out of the blue. Her uncle had always kept himself fit. He went for long walks along the white sandy beach, the sound of seagulls in his ears. He swam daily in a brilliantly blue sea, smooth as glass. To no avail. The truth was, no one knew what might happen next. The only certainty in life was death. Life was a circus; fate the ringmaster. Her uncle's illness demanded her presence. It was her turn to demonstrate her love.

Up ahead was another challenge. A procession of undertakers? A line of vehicles was crawling along as though they had all day to get to their destination. Where the heck *was* that? There were no shops or supermarkets nearby, only the unending rich red ochre fields lying fallow in vivid contrast with the striking green of the eternal cane. Planted in sugarcane, the North was an area of vibrant colour and great natural beauty. It occurred to her the procession might be heading to the cemetery via the South Pole.

Some five minutes later she arrived at the entrance to the hospital grounds. There was nothing to worry about, she kept telling herself. She had been assured of that by none other than Blaine Forrester, who had rung her with the news. She had known Blaine since her childhood. Her uncle thought the world of him. Fair to say Blaine was the son he never had. She *knew* she came first with her uncle, but his affection for Blaine, five years her senior, had always ruffled her feathers. She was *more* than Blaine, she had frequently reminded herself. He was the only son of good friends and neighbours. She was *blood*.

Blaine's assurances, his review of the whole situation, hadn't prevented her from feeling anxious. In the end Uncle Robert was all the family she had. Without him she would be alone.

Entirely alone.

The main gates were open, the entry made splendid by a pair of poincianas in sumptuous scarlet bloom. The branches of the great shade trees had been dragged down into their perfect umbrella shape by the sheer weight of the annual blossoming. For as far back as she could remember, the whole town of Forrester had waited for the summer flowering, as another town might wait for an annual folk festival. The royal poinciana, a native of Madagascar, had to be the most glorious ornamental tree grown in all subtropical and tropical parts of the world.

"Pure magic!" she said aloud.

It was her spontaneous response to the breathtaking display. Nothing could beat nature for visual therapy. As she watched, the breeze gusted clouds of spent blossom to the ground, forming a deep crimson carpet.

She parked, as waves of uncomplicated delight rolled over her. She loved this place. North of Capricorn was another world, an artist's dream. There had always been an artist's colony here. Some of the country's finest artists had lived and painted here, turning out their glorious land- and seascapes, scenes of island life. Uncle Robert had a fine body of their work at the house, including a beautiful painting of the district's famous Poinciana Road that led directly to Moonglade Estate. From childhood, poincianas had great significance for her. Psychic balm to a child's wounded heart and spirit, she supposed.

Vivid memories clung to this part of the world. The Good. The Bad. The Ugly. Memories were like ghosts that appeared in the night and didn't disappear at sunrise as they should. She knew the distance between memory and what really happened could be vast. Lesser memories were susceptible to reconstruction over the years. It was the *worst* memories one remembered best. The worst became deeply embedded.

Her memories were perfectly clear. They set her on edge the rare times she allowed them to flare up. Over the years she had developed many strategies to maintain her equilibrium. Self-control was her striking success. It was a marvellous disguise. One she wore well.

A light, inoffensive beep of a car horn this time brought her out of her reverie. She glanced in the rear-vision mirror, lifting an apologetic hand to the woman driver in the car behind her. She moved off to the parking bays on either side of the main entrance. Her eyes as a matter of course took in the variety of tropical shrubs, frangipani, spectacular Hawaiian hibiscus, and the heavenly perfumed oleanders that had been planted the entire length of the perimeter and in front of the bays. Like the poincianas, their hectic blooming was unaffected by the powerful heat. Indeed the heat only served to produce more ravishing displays. The mingled scents permeated the heated air like incense, catching at the nose and throat.

Tropical blooming had hung over her childhood; hung over her heart. High summer: hibiscus, heartbreak. She kept all that buried. A glance at the dash told her it was two o'clock. She had made good time. Her choice of clothing, her usual classic gear, would have been just right in the city. Not here. For the tropics she should have been wearing simple clothes, loose, light cotton. She was plainly overdressed. No matter. Her dress sense, her acknowledged stylishness, was a form of protection. To her mind it was like drawing a velvet glove over shattered glass.

Auxiliary buildings lay to either side of the main structure. There was a large designated area for ambulances only. She pulled into the doctors' parking lot. She shouldn't have parked there, but she excused herself on the grounds there were several other vacant spots. The car that had been behind her had parked in the visitors' zone. The occupant was already out of her vehicle, heading towards the front doors at a run.

"Better get my skates on," the woman called, with a friendly wave to Mallory as she passed. Obviously she was late, and by the look of it expected to be hauled over the coals.

There were good patients. And terrible patients. Mallory had seen both. Swiftly she checked her face in the rearview mirror. Gold filigrees of hair were stuck to her cheeks. Deftly she brushed them back. She had good, thick hair that was carefully controlled. No casual ponytail but an updated knot as primly elegant as an Edwardian chignon. She didn't bother to lock the doors, but made her way directly into the modern two-storied building.

The interior was brightly lit, with a smell like fresh laundry and none of the depressing clinical smells and the long, echoing hallways of the vast, impersonal city hospitals. The walls of the long corridor were off-white and hung with paintings she guessed were by local artists. A couple of patients in dressing gowns were wandering down the corridor to her left, chatting away brightly, as if they were off to attend an in-hospital concert. To her right a young male doctor, white coat flying, clipboard in hand, zipped into a room as though he didn't have a second to lose.

There was a pretty, part-aboriginal young nurse stationed at reception. At one end of the counter was a large Oriental vase filled with beautiful white, pink-speckled Asian lilies. Mallory dipped her head to catch their sweet, spicy scent.

"I'm here to see a patient, Robert James," she said, smiling as she looked up.

"Certainly, Dr. James." Bright, cheerful, accommodating. She was known. How?

An older woman with a brisk, no-nonsense air of authority, hurried towards reception. She too appeared pleased to see Mallory. Palm extended, she pointed off along the corridor. "Doctor Moorehouse is with Mr. James. You should be able to see him shortly, Dr. James. Would you like a cup of tea?"

Swiftly Mallory took note of the name tag. "A cup of tea would go down very nicely, Sister Arnold."

"I'll arrange it," said Sister. Their patient had a photograph of this young woman beside his bed. He invited everyone to take a look. *My beautiful niece, Mallory. Dr. Mallory James!*

Several minutes later, before she'd even sat down, Mallory saw one splendid-looking man stride up to reception. Six feet and over. Thoroughbred build. Early thirties. Thick head of crow-black hair. Clearly not one of the bit players in life.

Blaine!

The mere sight of him put her on high alert. Though it made perfect sense for him to be there, she felt her emotions start to bob up and down like a cork in a water barrel. For all her strategies, she had never mastered the knack of keeping focused with Blaine around. He knew her too well. That was the problem. He knew the number of times she had made a complete fool of herself. He knew all about her disastrous engagement. Her abysmal choice of a life partner. He had always judged her and found her wanting. Okay, they were friends, having known one another forever, but there were many downsides to their difficult, often stormy relationship. She might as well admit it. It was mostly her fault. So many times over the years she had been as difficult as she could be. It was a form of retaliation caused by a deep-seated grudge.

Blaine knew all about the years she had been under the care of Dr. Sarah Matthews, child psychologist and a leader in her field. The highly emotional, unstable years. He knew all about her dangerous habit of sleepwalking. Blaine knew far too much. Anyone would resent it. He wasn't a doctor, yet he knew her entire case history. For all that, Blaine was a man of considerable charisma. What was charisma anyway, she had often asked herself. Was one born with it or was it acquired over time? Did charismatic people provoke a sensual experience in everyone they met? She thought if they were like Blaine the answer had to be yes. One of Blaine's most attractive qualities was his blazing energy. It inspired confidence. Here was a man who could and did get things done.

Blaine was a big supporter of the hospital. He had property in all the key places. The Forrester family had made a fortune over the generations. They were descendants of George Herbert Forrester, an Englishman, already on his way to being rich before he left the colony of New South Wales to venture into the vast unknown territory which was to become the State of Queensland in 1859. For decades on end, the Forresters pretty well owned and ran the town. Their saving grace was that as employers they were very good to their workers, to the extent that everyone, right up to the present day, considered themselves part of one big happy Forrester family and acted accordingly.

She heard him speak to the nurse at reception. He had a compelling voice. It had a special quality to it. It exactly matched the man. She saw his aura. Her secret: She was able to see auras. Not of everyone. That would have been beyond anyone's ability to cope with. But *certain* people. Good and bad. She saw Blaine's now. The energy field that surrounded him was the familiar cobalt blue. She knew these auras were invisible to most people. She had no idea why she should see them, *feel* them, as *heat* waves. The gift, if it was one, hadn't been developed over the years. It had just always been there.

Once, to her everlasting inner cringe, she had confided her secret to Blaine. She was around fourteen at the time. There he was, so handsome, already making his mark, home from university. She remembered exactly where they were, lazing in the sun, down by Moonglade's lake. The moment she had stopped talking, he had propped himself up on his elbow, looking down at her with his extraordinary silver eyes.

"You're having me on!"
"No, I swear."
He burst out laughing. "Listen, kid. I'm cool with all your

tall tales and celestial travels, but we both know auras don't exist."

"They do. They do exist."

Her rage and disappointment in him had known no bounds. She had entrusted him with her precious secret and he, her childhood idol, had laughed her to scorn. No wonder she had gone off like a firecracker.

"Don't you dare call me a liar, Blaine Forrester. I see auras. I've seen your aura lots of times. Just because you can't see them doesn't mean they're not there. You're nothing but an insensitive, arrogant pig!"

He had made her *so* angry that even years later she still felt residual heat. She had wanted him to listen to her, to share. Instead he had ridiculed her. It might have been that very moment their easy, affectionate relationship underwent a dramatic sea change. Blaine, the friend she had so looked up to and trusted, had laughed at her. Called her a kid. She *did* see auras, some strong, some dim. It had something to do with her particular brain. One day, science would prove the phenomenon. In the meantime she continued to see auras that lasted maybe half a minute before they faded. Blaine-the-unbeliever's aura was as she had told him all those years ago, a cobalt blue. Uncle Robert's was pale green with a pinkish area over his heart. She couldn't see her own aura. She had seen her dying mother's black aura. Recognized what it meant. She had seen that black aura a number of times since.

A moment more and Blaine was making his way to the waiting room. Mercifully this one was empty, although Mallory could hear, farther along the corridor, a woman's voice reading a familiar children's story accompanied by children's sweet laughter. How beautiful was the laughter of children, as musical as wind chimes.

As Blaine reached the doorway she found herself standing up. Why she did was beyond her. The pity of it was she felt the familiar, involuntary flair of *excitement*. She was stuck with that, sadly. It would never go away. She extended her hand, hoping her face wasn't flushed. Hugs and air-kisses were long since out of the question between them. Yet, as usual, all her senses were on point. "Blaine."

"Mallory." He gave her a measured look, his fingers curling around hers. With a flush on her beautiful skin she looked radiant. Not that he was about to tell her. Mallory had no use whatever for compliments.

The mocking note in his voice wasn't lost on Mallory. She chose to ignore it. From long experience she was prepared for physical contact, yet as always she marvelled at the *charge*. It was pretty much like a mild electric shock. She had written it off as a case of static electricity. Physics. With his height, he made her willowy five feet eight seem petite. That gave him an extra advantage. His light grey eyes were in startling contrast to his hair and darkly tanned skin. Sculpted features and an air of sharp intelligence and natural authority made for an indelible impression. From long experience she knew Blaine sent women into orbit. It made her almost wish she was one of them. She believed the intensity of his gaze owed much to the luminosity of his eyes. Eyes like that would give anyone a jolt.

He gestured towards one of the long upholstered benches, as though telling her what to do. She *hated* that, as well. It was like he always knew the best course of action. She realized her reactions were childish, bred from long years of resenting him and his high-handed, taken-for-granted sense of superiority, but childish nevertheless. No one was perfect. He should have been kinder.

Blaine was fully aware of the war going on inside Mallory. He knew all about her anxieties, her complexities. He had first met her when she was seven, a pretty little girl with lovely manners. Mallory, the adult, was a woman to be reckoned with. Probably she would be formidable in old age. Right now, she was that odd combination of incredibly sexy and incredibly aloof. There was nothing even mildly flirtatious about her. Yet she possessed powers that he didn't understand. He wondered what would happen if she ever let those powers fly.

She was wearing a very stylish yellow jacket and skirt. City gear. Not a lot of women could get away with the colour. Her luxuriant dark gold hair was pulled back into some sort of knot. Her olive skin was flawless, her velvet-brown eyes set at a faint tilt. Mallory James was a beautiful woman, like her tragic mother before her. Brains and beauty had been bred into Mallory. Her academic brilliance had allowed her to take charge of her life. She had a PhD in child psychology. Close containment had become Mallory's way of avoiding transient sexual relationships and deep emotional involvement. Mallory made it very plain she was captain of her own ship.

The aftershock of their handshake was still running up Mallory's arm to her shoulder. She seized back control. She had spent years perfecting a cool façade. By now it was second nature. Only Blaine, to her disgust, had the power to disrupt her habitual poise. Yet there was something *real* between them; some deep empathy that inextricably tied them together. He to her, she to him. She was aware of the strange disconnect between their invariably charged conversations and a *different* communication she refused to investigate.

"I'm worried about Uncle Robert," she said briskly. She supposed he could have interpreted it as accusatory. "You told me it was a *mild* heart attack, Blaine. I thought he would be home by now. Yet he's still in hospital."

"He's in for observation, Mallory. No hurry." *Here we go again*, he thought.

"Anything else I should know?" She studied him coolly. The handsomeness, the glowing energy, the splendid physique.

"Ted will fill you in."

"So there's nothing you can tell me?" Her highly sensitive antennae were signalling there was more to come.

"Not really." His light eyes sparkled in the rays of sunlight that fell through the high windows.

"So why do I have this feeling you're keeping something from me?"

Blaine nearly groaned aloud. As usual she was spot-on, only he knew he had to work his way up to full disclosure. "Mallory, it's essential to Robb's recovery for you to be *here,* not in Brisbane. He's slowed down of recent times, but he never said there was anything to worry about. It now appears he has a heart condition. Angina."

"But he never told me." She showed her shock and dismay.

"Nor me. Obviously he didn't want it to be known."

Without thinking, she clutched his arm as if he might have some idea of walking away from her. He was wearing a short-sleeved cotton shirt, a blue-and-white check, with his jeans, so she met with suntanned, warm skin and hard muscle. She should have thought of that. Blaine had such physicality it made her stomach contract. He further rattled her by putting his hand on top of hers.

"You believe I have a moral obligation to look out for my uncle as he looked after me?"

"I'm not here to judge you, Mallory," he said smoothly.

"Never mind about that. I'm always under surveillance." Blaine had established the habit of meeting up with her whenever he was in Brisbane on business, which was often. His lawyers, accountants, stockbrokers, among others, were all stationed in the state capital. He made sure she could always be contacted. He was highly esteemed by her uncle, for whom he clearly stood in.

His hand dropped away first. It had made her uncomfortable feeling the strength of his arm and the warmth of his skin, but she wasn't about to waste time fretting about it.

"That's in *your* head, Mallory. It's not true. More like I've tried my hardest to be a good friend to you."

You difficult woman, you. He didn't need to say it; Mallory heard it loud and clear.

"Anyway, you're here now. You can give Robb your undivided attention for a few days."

"Whatever you say, Blaine. You're the boss." Heat was spreading through her. In the old days she had let it control her. Not now. As Doctor Mallory James, she was used to being treated with respect. "Uncle Robert and I are in constant touch, as you well know. Anyway, he has *you*," she tacked on sweetly. "Always ready to help. The figure of authority in the town."

"Do I detect a lick of jealousy?"

"Jealousy!" She gasped. "That's a charge and a half."

"Okay, make it sibling rivalry, even if we aren't siblings. You can't rule it out. I've known Robb all my life. My parents loved him. He was always welcome at our home. I remember the first time you turned up. A perfectly sweet little girl *in those days*, with long blond hair tied back with a wide blue ribbon. My father said later, 'Those two should be painted, Claudia and her beautiful little daughter.'"

"That never happened." A flush had warmed Mallory's skin. She wished she could dash it away.

"I noticed like everyone else how closely you resembled your mother," Blaine said more gently.

"Ah, the fatal resemblance! It was extraordinary and it impacted too many lives." She broke off at the sound of approaching footsteps. Sister Arnold was returning with tea.

Blaine moved to take the tray from her. "Thank you, Sister."

"Would you like a cup yourself, Mr. Forrester?"

How many times had Mallory heard just that worshipful tone? Nothing would ever be too much trouble for Blaine Forrester; tea, coffee, scones, maybe a freshly baked muffin?

"I'm fine, thank you, Sister." He gave her a smile so attractive it could sell a woman into slavery.

"You could bring another cup, Sister, if you don't mind," said Mallory. There was really something about Blaine that was very dangerous to women.

"No trouble at all." Sister Arnold gave Blaine a look that even a blind woman would interpret as nonprofessional.

"I don't drink tea," Blaine mentioned as she bustled away.

"At this point, who cares? Sister likes bringing it. Makes her day."

He ignored the jibe as too trivial to warrant comment. "You drove all this way?"

She nodded. "One stop. It would have been a whole lot quicker to fly, but I don't enjoy air travel, as you know." She was borderline claustrophobic but halfway to conquering it.

"That's your Mercedes out front?"

"It is." She had worked long and hard to pay it off. "I love my car. You did *assure* me Uncle Robert was in no danger."

"With care and the right medication, Robb has many good years left in him"

"I hope so." Mallory released a fervent breath.

"Ah, here's Sister back with my tea."

"Don't forget to give her your dazzling smile."

"How odd you noticed," he said, his sparkling eyes full on hers.

An interlude followed, filled with the usual ping-pong of chat, largely saturated with sarcasm, most of it hers. Dr. Edward Moorehouse, looking like an Einstein incarnation with his white bush of hair and a walrus moustache, hurried into the waiting room. A highly regarded cardiac specialist, he possessed a sweetness of heart and an avuncular charm.

"Ah, Mallory, Blaine!" He saluted them, looking from one to the other with evident pleasure. His head was tilted to one side, much like a bird's, his dark eyes bright with more than a hint of mischief. "How lovely to see you together. I hear such good things about you, Mallory."

Mallory kissed him gently on both cheeks, feeling a sense of warmth and homecoming. "Doctor Sarah set my feet on my chosen path."

"Bless her."

Dr. Sarah Matthews had guided Mallory through her severe childhood traumas: her terrible grief over the violent, sudden death of her adored mother, which she had witnessed, the later abandonment of her by her father, compounded by irrational feelings of guilt that she had lived when her beautiful mother had died.

"Wonderful woman, Sarah!" Moorehouse's voice was tinged with sadness. Sarah Matthews had died of lung cancer a couple of years previously, though she had never smoked a cigarette in her life. "We will always have a job for you if you ever come back to us, Mallory. No one has taken Sarah's place with the same degree of success. There are always cases needing attention, even here in this paradise."

She was aware of that. "Blaine tells me Uncle Robert has had a heart condition for some time. I didn't know that."

"Robb wouldn't have wanted to worry you." Moorehouse darted a glance at Blaine, then back to Mallory. "He has his medication. Robb is the most considerate man I know," he said in his soothing manner.

Mallory wasn't sidetracked. "He *should* have told me. I needed to know."

"Don't agitate yourself, Mallory. With care and keeping on his meds, Robb has some good years left to him."

"Some?" She had to weigh that answer very carefully.

"All being well." Ted Moorehouse spoke with a doctor's inbuilt caution. "You must be longing to see him. I'll take you to his room."

"I'll stay here." Blaine glanced at Mallory. "You'll want to see Robert on your own."

"I appreciate that, Blaine," she said gracefully. "Give us ten minutes and then come through."

They found Robert James sitting up in bed, propped up by pillows. An ecstatic smile lit his still handsome face the moment Mallory walked in the door. As a consequence, Mallory's vision started to cloud. Outside his room she had steeled herself, concerned at how he might look after his heart attack. Now his appearance reassured her. She felt like a little girl again, a bereaved child. Uncle Robert was the one who had been there for her, taking her in. She couldn't bear the thought of his leaving her.

The ones you love best, die.

She knew that better than anyone.

*   *   *

Robert James, gazing at the figure of his adored niece, felt wave after wave of joy bubbling up like a fountain inside his chest. She had come back to him. Claudia's daughter. His niece. His brother's child. His family. He was deeply conscious of how much he had missed Mallory these past years, although they kept in close touch. He had accepted her decision to flee the town where he had raised her. She had strong reasons, and he accepted them. Besides, clever young woman that she was, she had to find her place in the larger world. He was so proud of Mallory and her accomplishments. Proud he had been her mentor. His whole being, hitherto on a downward spiral, sparked up miraculously.

"Mallory, darling girl!" He held out his arms to gather her in. What he really felt like doing was getting out of bed and doing a little dance.

"Uncle Robert." Mallory swallowed hard on the lump in her throat. She wasn't about to cry in front of him, though she felt alarm at the lack of colour in his aura. Love for him consumed her. He looked on the gaunt side, but resplendent in stylish silk pyjamas. Robert James was elegant wherever he was, in hospital, in private. Like her father, he was a bit of a dandy. There were violet shadows under his eyes, hollows beneath his high cheekbones and at the base of his throat. But there was colour in his cheeks, even if it was most probably from excitement. He had lost much-needed weight, along with strength and vitality; hence his diminished aura.

"It's so wonderful to see you, sweetheart, but you didn't have to come all this way. Ted says I'm fine."

"You *are* fine, Robb," Ted Moorehouse said quietly. He knew how much his friend loved his niece. Her presence would do him a power of good. "I'll leave you two together. You can take Robb home around this time tomorrow, Mallory." He half turned at the door. "I expect you're staying for a day or two?"

Mallory tightened her hold on her uncle's thin hand, meeting his eyes. "Actually I've taken extended leave."

"Why that's wonderful, Mallory." Moorehouse beamed his approval. "Just what the doctor ordered." He lifted a benedictory hand as he headed out the door.

"Extended leave! I feel on top of the world already." Robert's fine dark eyes were brimming with an invalid's tears.

Mallory bowed her head humbly at her uncle's intense look of gratitude. It was *she* who had every reason to be grateful. She pulled up a chair and sat down at the bedside. Her touch featherlight, she smoothed his forehead with gentle fingertips, let them slide down over his thin cheek. "I'm so sorry if I've hurt you with my long absence, Uncle Robert. I know Blaine finds it so. He's outside, by the way."

"He's always there when you need him." Robert's voice was full of the usual pride and affection. "To be honest, I don't know what I would have done without him. He's been splendid, a real chip off the old block. Not that D'Arcy ever got to grow old."

Mallory bowed her head. She wasn't the only one who had lost a beloved parent. Blaine too had suffered. D'Arcy Forrester had been killed leading a cleanup party after a severe cyclone. He had trodden on fallen power lines that had been camouflaged by a pile of palm fronds. His passing had been greatly mourned in the town. The reins had been passed into Blaine's capable hands.

Robert James's hollowed-out gaze rested on his niece. "Does Nigel know about me?"

Mallory's smile barely wavered. "I've left messages. I'm sure he'll respond."

"I won't count on it." Robert spoke wryly. "Stripped of the mask of learnedness, my brother is not a caring man. What heart he had went with your mother. I would have liked to see him, all the same. We *are* blood."

Unease etched itself on Mallory's face. "Goodness, Uncle Robert, you're not dying." She tightened her grip as if to hold him forever. "You've got plenty more good years left to you. I'm here now. Father will be in contact, I'm sure." She was certain her father had received her messages. But her father hated confronting issues like illness and death.

Some minutes later, Blaine walked through the door, his eyes taking in the heartwarming sight of uncle and niece lovingly holding hands. "How goes it?"

"Wonderful, thank you, Blaine," Robert responded, eyes bright. "Ted says I can come home tomorrow."

"That's great news. I can pick you up in the Range Rover. To make it easy for Mallory, I can pick her up on the way."

So it was arranged, and they left the room.

* * *

She didn't so much walk as glide on those long, elegant legs, Blaine thought. Mallory moved like a dancer; every twist and turn, every smooth pivot. It was high time he dropped the bombshell and then stood well back for the fallout. He knew Robb hadn't told her. Robb simply wasn't up to it. It was part of Robb's avoidance program.

"Something I should tell you, Mallory." He hoped if she was going to shoot the messenger she aimed high.

"I *knew* there was something." Mallory came to an abrupt halt.

"Your psychic powers?" he suggested, that irritating quirk to his handsome mouth.

"Why don't you double up with laughter? What powers I have— which you *don't believe* is true— do work. I've been picking up vibes that something wasn't right. I can see by your face you'd prefer not to be having the upcoming conversation." Normally she spoke quietly. She was quiet with her movements as well. She never sought to draw attention to herself, but with Blaine her usually controlled manner became by comparison nearly theatrical.

"How right you are. I don't think you could guess, so I'll get right to it. Jason Cartwright has a job at Moonglade. On the farm."

The shock was so great she felt like ducking for cover.

Blaine showed his concern. "Hey, are you okay?"

For a moment she was too dumbfounded to reply. "Okay? I'm the expert on okay. I'm actually delirious with joy. Jason at the farm! What luck!" Her blood pressure was definitely soaring well above her usual spot-on 119/76.

He didn't relish this job, but he had promised Robb he would bring Mallory up to date. Robb tended to pull in the favours. "I'm sorry to spring it on you. Robb has never told you for his own reasons, but it's something you obviously need to know now you're here."

Take your time.

Stare into space for a minute.

She felt more like shouting, only that would be so utterly, utterly unlike Dr. Mallory James. "I love Uncle Robert dearly, but we both know he evades difficult issues like the plague. I *knew* he was keeping something from me."

"Your psychic powers didn't fill you in?"

"Oh, bugger off, Blaine." Abruptly she stalked off to her car, unlocking the doors with a press on the remote. She felt like driving back the way she came.

Blaine caught up with her with ease. "We can handle this, Mallory."

"*We?*" she huffed, rounding on him. "*We* will, will we? I love that. Your offer of support only grates."

"It's well meant. I've another surprise for you."

Her dark eyes flashed. "Don't hang about. Get it out. It's a bigger surprise than Jason working at the farm?"

For a woman who hated to lose her cool, Mallory's dark eyes gave Mallory, the enigma, away. They were *passionate* eyes. "He *runs* it," Blaine bit off. "No point in stretching things out."

She tried to find words. None came. "Well, he's had such a rotten time, he deserves a break," she said finally.

"I share your dismay."

"Then why didn't you stop it?" She was trying without success to dampen the burn inside her. "You can do *anything* when you want to. I've seen plenty of evidence of that over the years. You're the fixer. You run the town."

"I've never said that."

"You don't have to. Does the Queen tell everyone she's the Queen? She doesn't have to."

"Are you hearing yourself?" He too was firing up. "Be fair. It was Robb's decision, Mallory. It was never going to be mine. I couldn't take matters out of his hands. Robb owns Moonglade and the business. I've never been a fan of Jason's, but he's not a criminal."

"He *is* a criminal!" Mallory declared fiercely. "He betrayed me. He betrayed his family, Uncle Robert, even the town. That's criminal in my book. Honestly, Blaine, this is too much."

He agreed, but he wasn't about to stoke the flames. "I can't expect you to be happy about it. He's good at the job. He works hard."

Mallory shook her head. "The golden boy! That makes it okay for my married ex-fiancé to live and work on the doorstep? I suppose I can be grateful he wasn't invited to live in the house. Why couldn't Uncle Robert tell me himself? I don't give a damn how efficient Jason is. Uncle Robert—" She broke off in disgust. "It's the avoidance syndrome. It's rife among men." She propped herself against her car, in case she slid ignominiously to the ground. "Why does chaos follow me?"

"You're doing okay," he said briskly.

She waved off his comment. "What is *wrong* with Uncle Robb's thinking?"

"Obviously, it's different from yours."

"Ss-o?" she almost stuttered.

"If someone's decisions are different from our own, then we tend to assume it doesn't make a lot of sense."

"There's nothing wrong with my thinking, thank you." She became aware she was beating an angry tattoo on the concrete with the toe of her shoe. This wasn't like her. Not like her at all. Blaine found the terrible weak spot in her defences. "You didn't understand Uncle Robert's decision, did you?"

"The milk of human kindness? Blessed are the merciful, and all that?"

"I love the way you guys stick together."

"Oh, come off it, Mallory," he said, exasperated.

"We never know people, do we? Even the people closest to us. We always miss something. Uncle Robert needed to tell me. *You* of all people should know that."

"Damn it, Blaine, Jason's working at Moonglade is an outrage. It chills my heart. So don't stand there looking like business as usual."

He rubbed the back of his tanned neck. "It won't help to see it like that, Mallory. It's a done deal. You'd moved on. You didn't come back. It was well over six years ago."

"An astonishing amount of time. So you're saying *I'm* the one who is acting badly? Or am I an idiot for asking?"

"I don't think you're likely to hear the word 'idiot' in connection with you in a lifetime. Robb has a notoriously kind heart. He gave your ex-fiancé a job after it became apparent Harry Cartwright had disowned his only son. Robb is a very compassionate man."

"A sucker for a sob story, you mean. Okay, okay, *I* was a sob story. A seven-year-old kid who had lost her mother. A kid who was abandoned by her greatly admired, gutless father because I'm the spitting image of my mother. He couldn't look at me. I might have had two heads. I was his little daughter so much in need of a father's comfort, but my appearance totally alienated him. It was like I should have had plastic surgery, changed the colour of my hair, popped in baby-blue contact lenses. Ah, what the hell!" She broke off, ashamed of her rant.

"Mallory, I can't think of a single soul who didn't find your father's behaviour deplorable. You had a tough time, but you've come through with flying colours."

"An illusion I've managed to create."

"We all create illusions. I do get how you feel."

She raised her face to his, not bothering to hide her agitation. "How do you get it? Selma didn't run off from your wedding, so be grateful for that. Jason was an assassin. He stabbed me in the back, right on the eve of our wedding, remember? You should, you were there. You're *always* there, letting me know what a fool I am. Will you ever forget how the news of Kathy Burch's pregnancy spread like wildfire around the town? The disgrace. The humiliation. The shame. To make it worse, Uncle Robert had spent a fortune ensuring a fairy-tale wedding for me."

"I did warn you."

She felt the screws tighten. "Yeah, prescient old you! You must get great satisfaction out of knowing everything you said about Jason came true."

"He wasn't the most desirable candidate for your hand. Certainly not the husband of choice."

"Not your choice for me."

"Not Robb's choice either, even if he avoided saying so, which is a great pity, but seriously not worth getting into now. It didn't make me *happy* to say what I said then."

"I don't believe that for one moment. You relished the breakup. I was under so much stress, but you, superior old you, had to punch my stupidity home."

An answering heat of anger was rising in him. A certain amount of conflict with Mallory was par for the course. "How unfair can you get? If I'd told you I thought Jason Cartwright was absolutely *perfect*, you might have broken off the engagement."

She stared at him, wondering in consternation if he had spoken a truth. "There's always friction between us, isn't there?" she said, angrily puffing at a stray lock of her hair. "Bottled up forces."

"That's what *you* want, Mallory. Not me." Blaine stared down at her. Radiance had a way of playing around Mallory. The hot sun was picking out the gold strands in her hair and at her temples. The delicate bones of her face he found not only endearing but intensely erotic.

"Jason was kicked out of his home and the thriving family real estate business for reasons unknown. Was it money?" Mallory pondered. "Money causes big problems. Were the twins robbing their father on the side? Surely Uncle Robert pressed Jason for some explanation?"

"None forthcoming to this day." Blaine fixed a glance on her narrow, tapping foot.

She stopped the tapping. "You've always been able to get to the bottom of things."

"Wasn't my place, Mallory, as I said."

"Well, I can't accept you don't have *some* idea as to what the breakup was all about. You have your little network. All the businessmen in town want to hook up with you. They all know Harry. What about the grapevine?"

"Oddly, the breakup hasn't become the talk of the town. It's a mystery, destined to remain so."

She gave another dismissive wave of her hand. "I don't like mysteries, especially when they impact on my life. His parents doted on Jason. Could the fallout have been because of *me*? That would make me very uncomfortable indeed."

"I think not."

"How can you be so sure?"

"I know that much, Mallory."

She felt another quick surge of anger. "Of course you do, and a whole lot more you're not telling. Jason married Kathy Burch. They have a little girl."

"Her name is Ivy, a cute little kid. Kathy, however, is a very subdued young woman these days. Marriage and motherhood have—"

"Taken their toll?"

"The short answer is yes. Kathy is very much under Jessica's thumb."

She took a deep breath. Counted to ten. "A bigger bombshell is coming? Jessica is still on the scene?"

"Try to pry her away from her brother," Blaine said, his tone bone dry.

"Can no one kill her off? Or at least start looking into it?"

"No way of doing it without landing in jail," Blaine said laconically. "Those two were always joined at the hip. Jason and Kathy live in the old manager's bungalow, by the way. Robert remodeled it for them."

Mallory put her fingertips to her aching temples. "I didn't come prepared for these disclosures, Blaine. To think of all the phone calls, the e-mails, the visits, and never a word."

"Not so surprising, is it?"

She shook her head. "Not really. We both know Uncle Robert avoids unpleasantness. It's his problem area. As for *you*! You too left me completely in the dark."

"Mallory, I couldn't go over Robb's head."

"I had rights, didn't I?"

"You left, Mallory, telling us you were never coming back."

"Who would blame me? You're not the most compassionate man in the world, are you?"

"Compassion wasn't, still isn't, what you wanted," he said testily.

Mallory gave up. She would never win with Blaine. "I can't believe the Cartwrights would turn their backs on their only grandchild. Kathy might remain the outsider, but cutting off the little girl, the innocent victim, their own flesh and blood? The Marge Cartwright I remember was a nurturing woman."

"Maybe Jason is hitting back at his parents by not allowing them to see the child. She has a few problems apparently."

"Problems? What sort of problems?" Immediately Mallory started ticking off childhood disorders in her head.

"Health problems, and I believe she's a little wild. The whole town knows. Kathy is always at the hospital with her."

"How very worrying." Mallory's stance had softened considerably. "Is the child on medication? There are so many underlying reasons for behavioural problems. Sometimes it can be hard for a GP to differentiate. Kids are hyper for a wide range of reasons."

"I'm sure you're right, Doctor James."

Ah, the suavity of his tone! "Helping problematic children is my area, Blaine," she reminded him sharply. "I'd like to point out, while we're on the subject, I didn't allow bitterness over what happened to me and Jason to eat me away. What's past is past."

"Faulkner didn't see it that way."

"Okay, the past is never past. That way of yours of constantly having the last word drives me crazy."

"As I've suggested, it could be your bad case of 'sibling' rivalry. You were lucky you didn't marry Jason. He didn't break your heart."

"Did Selma break yours?"

He only shrugged. "Forget Selma. Look, I'm not in the mood for this, Mallory."

"Then you're welcome to go on your way. I'm not stopping you." She tilted her chin.

"Take a chill pill, why don't you."

She flared up. "Chill pill? I don't pop pills." She had been on antidepressants for some years. Occasionally she had panic attacks, but she worked to contain them without medication.

"Oh, for God's sake, Mallory! Why do you work so hard to misunderstand me? You're a psychologist. You know all about chill pills to control moods. I know this is difficult. If it helps, Cartwright is working hard. *Jessica* too."

For a split second she allowed her shoulders to droop. Then she straightened. No way was Blaine going to see her crumple. She'd do that when she was alone.

"Jessica Cartwright mightn't be a bucket of fun, but she's extremely competent," he went on. "She's far better than Jason at getting the best out of the staff."

"That's her big rap, is it? Jessica Cartwright gets the best out of the staff. Does she do it with a whip? Jessica was the nastiest kid in the school. She tormented the life out of Kathy Burch, when Kathy had suffered enough with that appalling father. Dare I ask how she wrangled the job?"

"Good question."

"With no good answer. Uncle Robert never liked her. He once called her a little monster."

"Tell me who did like her? Being pleasant never caught up with Jessica. She needed a job. The prospect of her finding work in town was uncertain at best."

"Most people had had kids in school with Jessica," Mallory said tartly.

"She mightn't have a winning personality, but Jason's life doesn't seem to be complete without her."

"Repressed development. Jessica is the alpha twin. She's always been in charge. But Jason is a married man now. If Jessica is around she probably spends her time ensuring every day is a real *bad* day for her sister-in-law. It's cruel for Jason to subject his wife to Jessica's TLC. God forbid he does it on purpose." Mallory felt up to her neck in unwelcome disclosures. "She's not his identical twin. They don't share identical genetic material. Jason was as pleasant as Jessica was downright nasty. Having said that, twinship is a deeply symbiotic relationship. I hope it's not too rude to ask, but what now? Is there a way out?"

"Not at the moment. Jessica lives in an apartment in town."

"I expect you own the complex?"

"I expect I do," he said.

"Modesty doesn't come in your size, does it?"

"If you say so, *dear* Mallory," he drawled. "To try to balance the good with the bad, Jessica has stuck by her brother."

"She'd stick with him if he were a total nutter. I really liked the Cartwrights."

"And they *loved* you." He went heavy on the *loved*.

"It was what it was," she said soberly. "So you got me here knowing all this?"

"I got you here for *Robert*. You owe him."

Memory after memory was sidling up. All of them full of angst. "I do so love you when you're righteous!"

"Me, righteous?" He spread his shapely hands.

"That's one of your big problems, Blaine. You're most righteous when you're in the wrong. And this is wrong."

"Would you have come back had you known?" He pinned her with his luminous eyes.

"So you deliberately kept me in the dark?"

"What would you have done had I told you the truth?"

She averted her gaze. "You don't know the workings of my mind, Blaine."

"You don't know mine, either."

"What's that supposed to mean?"

"You're smart. You'll figure it out. One piece of advice. Take it slowly."

She searched his face. Blaine was a central part of her life, but hunkering down inside her bolt hole had become a habit. "You make that sound like I could be steering into dangerous waters."

"And so you could be."

"They know I'm coming?"

Blaine nodded. "I expect they're feeling their own brand of trepidation. But life has moved on. *You* have moved on, Mallory. You're Doctor James now, a highly regarded professional in your field. You could even be of help to the child."

The thought took the edge off her upset. "Only I'm certain Jason and his wife wouldn't want any help from me. Jessica was *never* my friend."

"I did tell you that as well."

"You did indeed." Between the heat and her sizzling emotions, she felt compelled to get away from him. "You know I've always thought you a complete—"

He cut her off, opening her car door. "No need to say it, Mallory. I can fill in the dots. And it wasn't *always*. Once we were good pals, until puberty got in the way."

"Puberty? Whose puberty?" she demanded, incensed.

"Why, yours, of course. I'm not a fool, Mallory. I know you hate it, but I know you too well."

"You'll need to do a lot of catch-up." With practised grace, she swivelled her long, elegant legs as she settled into the driver's seat. "You find this funny?" She caught the glint in his eyes.

"Not at all. I just hope you're relatively okay with it."

"Like I'm relatively okay with a Category Five cyclone. What time tomorrow?"

"Say eleven o'clock. Robert has a new housekeeper. Mrs. Rawlings. She lost her husband, Jeff, to cancer."

She nodded. "Uncle Robert did manage to tell me. I'm sorry. He told me plenty about your goings-on as well. We do so know he thinks of you as the son he never had. What did go wrong between you and Selma, anyway?" Her voice was edged with malice, when malice didn't come naturally to her. "I would have thought she was madly in love with you."

"You've managed to make that sound like one would have to wonder why."

"Just trying to spin your wheels. Besides, I didn't think you cared all that much what I thought."

"I'll let that one go as well. It was Selma who decided against an engagement," he offered with no loss of his iron-clad composure.

"It was the other way around, I fancy. She loved you, but you found you didn't love her, or not enough to get married. Had you a new conquest in mind?"

He made to close her door. "Let's swap stories at another time, shall we, Mallory?"

"Nothing in it for you, Blaine. I'm a closed book."

"Unknowable to everyone but *me*."

She could have cheerfully slapped him. Instead she found herself tightening her body against the odd tumbling inside her. "I assume that's your arrogance talking?"

"Not entirely. See you tomorrow."

He shut her door.

He walked away.

He didn't look back.

USA Today bestselling author **Margaret Way** has written more than 130 books, many of them International Bestsellers. She has been published in 114 countries and 34 languages. Her novels are set in her beloved Australia, where she was born and lives to this day. Her stories always contain the beauty and rugged nature of the rural and Outback Australia, as well as the rainforests and coral reefs of Northern Queensland.